Stiletto
Silver

CW00751495

A GREAT COLLECTION OF EROTIC NOVELS FEATURING FEMALE DOMINANTS

If you like one you will probably like the rest

A NEW TITLE EVERY MONTH

Stiletto Readers Service
c/o Silver Moon Books Ltd
109A Roundhay Road
Leeds, LS8 5AJ

http://www.electronicbookshops.com

Silver Moon Books of Leeds and New York are in no way connected with
Silver Moon Books of London

If you like one of our books you will probably
like them all!

Stiletto Reader Services

c/o Silver Moon Books Ltd
109A Roundhay Road
Leeds, LS8 5AJ

http://www.electronicbookshops.com

New authors welcome
Please send submissions to
STILETTO
Silver Moon Books Ltd.
PO Box 5663
Nottingham
NG3 6PJ

MILITARY DISCIPLINE first published 2001,copyright ANNA GRANT

The right of Anna Grant to be identified as the author of this book has been asserted in accordance with Section 77
and 78 of the Copyrights and Patents Act 1988

MILITARY DISCIPLINE
by
Anna Grant

This is fiction - In real life always practise safe sex!

"MILITARY DISCIPLINE"

A collection of six short stories

by

Anna Grant

As she struggled to escape her captor Debbie wondered how the hell she had got herself into this mess in the first place. She lay face down in the mud with the boot of her hated rival Jennifer Trent in the middle of her back and her gun trained on her quivering buttocks with no possibility of escaping her clutches.

She tried to look over her shoulder at the woman that had caught her but was rewarded with a shot at point-blank range from Jennifer's feared weapon. The pop of the report was instantly followed by an explosion of agony in Debbie's left buttock as the bright yellow paintball burst over her tight combat trousers.

Debbie screamed with shock for the pain across her bottom was simply excruciating at such close range. She looked up again at the woman that held her down like an animal in the dirt, hoping that the shot had been a mistake but all she saw was Jennifer laughing at her misfortune.

Debbie turned to put her face back onto the ground sighing to herself as she realised that she was now entirely at the woman's mercy. How could she have been so stupid as to fall into the hands of this sadistic bitch when she had been the one Debbie had been hunting in the first place? Come to think of it why had Debbie even turned up at this God forsaken wood in the middle of North Yorkshire to go paintballing in the first place?

Of course it had all been Jennifer's idea, who as the new office manager had decided that a team building adventure was needed for the staff. She was the new girl in the office so, in an effort to stamp her authority on her new colleagues, she had organised this trip to a desolate and remote wood in the North, to go paintballing.

Unsurprisingly all the lads had loved the idea, especially as it gave them the chance to show off their prowess in front of the diminutive blonde whom they had all fallen for. It made Debbie sick the way they had all drooled over her since the day she had arrived.

The woman was attractive it had to be admitted, with her voluptuous figure squeezed indecently snugly into her power suit. The five-inch stiletto heels that she wore certainly gave her a taller appearance as well as heightening her sex appeal for all the males in the organisation, including even the young lads who delivered the post in the mornings.

Debbie had watched them drooling over her as she went about her daily tasks which seemed mainly to consist of changing everything to suit her purposes. The men had practically fallen over themselves to cater for her every need, leaving Debbie seething at the presence of this interloper in what she regarded, as her office.

She did not think that it was jealousy but before Jennifer had graced the scene Debbie had been the belle of the ball. Her long dark hair combined with her dazzling good looks had attracted a lot of attention but mainly it had been her deep brown eyes that had held her potential suitors spellbound.

All the male members of staff as well as one or two of the women lusted after her. She received many tempting offers from colleagues of both sexes, some of which she had even taken up. She had gone back with her various temporary partners to indulge in a mind-boggling range of sexual liaisons. One man, who had since left the firm, had persuaded her to dress up as an old-fashioned school mistress in order that she could thrash him senseless with a long whippy cane. She had made him cry like a baby in his school uniform after a few extremely vicious strokes so the session had ended rather prematurely much to Debbie's disappointment.

A woman who still worked on the floor below Debbie's

6

had taken their date together as a chance to tie her spread-eagled on her bed absolutely stark naked. Debbie had been thrilled at first to have the tables turned, particularly when her tormentor had produced a long ostrich feather with which to tickle her confined victim. However, Debbie had changed her mind about the whole thing when the woman had climbed onto her with her thighs on either side of her head. She balked at being made to lick the woman's pussy for she could see her juices dribbling from her gaping sex. She liked the taste of her own arousal but she refused to lap at this woman's for there was a limit to how far she would submit.

The dalliance had ended once Debbie had been released but there were many other people willing to share their fantasies with her. However, after being bound helplessly to another woman's bed she had always felt more comfortable if she had the upper hand in the relationships.

It had been the men oddly enough who wanted to submit themselves to her various forms of control. This had given her many opportunities to brush up on her techniques of dominating what she considered to be weak-willed men. She had used them to gain access to fancy restaurants or to accumulate a fascinating array of glittering trinkets that the humbled and grateful men had bestowed upon her. She had simply used them and taken what she could before she moved onto her next prey. She had never allowed a man or a woman a second chance; snubbing them brutally if they dared ask.

Her supply of willing victims however, had dried up the moment that the slut Jennifer had arrived with her bossy ways. All her previous lovers had deserted her in a thus far fruitless quest to get into the new girl's panties.

Debbie had tried to respond by tarting herself up with ever more revealing dresses complemented by exquisite make-up, but all to no avail. No one was interested in her any more for

7

they were all after the wonderful newcomer Jennifer.

What made things worse for Debbie was the fact that she was sure that the others in the office were all telling Jennifer about their sessions with her. She knew that they were probably calling her a whore behind her back, but there was nothing that she could do about it.

She had tried to carry on with her work as if nothing had happened, attempting to hide her obvious dislike for this interloper. She ignored her as much as she dared although this was proving to be very difficult as Jennifer was her immediate boss. It was galling for Debbie to have to work under the woman who had knocked her off her perch as queen of the office. She could no longer simply pick out the ones she wanted to abuse but had to humbly serve a woman whom she was rapidly coming to hate.

She boiled with anger every time Jennifer spoke to her colleagues or bustled through the office so full of her own importance. But when Jennifer actually dared to order her about Debbie squirmed with frustration at having to comply, even though she really felt like telling the tramp to get lost.

Things got even worse when Jennifer began to organise little staff events 'to boost morale' as she called it. Pubs or clubs were visited to start with, although the first trips were by no means compulsory which meant that Debbie could at least stay away. However, Jennifer's latest brainwave had resulted in a trip that all the office had been forced to take part in. She had sold the idea to the head of the company who had thought that it was a brilliant plan to promote team work within the firm.

So Debbie had reluctantly turned up at this camp in the middle of the countryside to play her part in the team. She had worn the skimpiest of summer dresses of light cotton along with dainty high-heeled sandals. She had also decided against wearing any underwear because she didn't want to spoil the lines of her snug fitting dress. She had wanted to make an impression amongst her former admirers with her striking appearance but her plan had backfired for she had not been told to wear rough clothes for the event. Jennifer had conveniently forgotten to tell her that she would get very muddy as well as covered in paint.

They had been given camouflage suits of course but Debbie had brought nothing to wear under them. In order to put the strange uniform on she had to face the humiliating ordeal of removing her dress to reveal her naked body to the rest of the team.

There were no changing rooms so she huddled in a corner as she got changed, facing away from the rest. Even though she tried to hide herself as best she could Debbie knew that the others were leering at her body which most of them knew so well already.

As she pulled on the trousers of the uniform she realised that they were far too tight for her. She pushed her legs into the trousers, quickly pulling them up to restrict the view the others could have of her exposed pussy. They clung to her thighs like cling film, outlining her muscles as she bent to retrieve her top. Debbie forced her full body into the coarse material which immediately squashed her ample breasts painfully against her chest. As she tied up all the loose strings of her restrictive outfit she realised that she did not have any boots to run around in the woods in. The wonderful Jennifer however had come to her aid with a pair of enormous boots in her hand. They were far too big but Debbie didn't want to attract any more attention to her misfortune than she already had. She simply pulled the boots on, lacing them as tightly as she could so as not to fall over when she walked.

The last part of the uniform was something that looked like a gas mask with straps to secure it to the wearer's head. Debbie tentatively put on the mask which immediately steamed up as she tried to breathe through it. She hadn't relished the prospect of wearing the device but the instructor had warned them that they should never take it off once they left the safe zone of the reception area. Therefore she kept it on as she trooped after the others out towards the battle zone and to start the first war game.

She had been picked for blue team, which she happily noted was opposite to Jennifer for it meant that at least she had the legitimate chance to shoot her. As Debbie picked up her air-powered paintballing gun she began to relish the thought of firing a paint pellet straight into in Jennifer's smug face. Perhaps, if she could catch her when Jennifer's gun was empty she would even have the chance to take the little bitch prisoner as the rules had suggested,. There was the possibility of treating her as a prisoner of war which would offer the perfect opportunity to get her own back on the new belle of the office.

She had followed the rest of blue team towards a small hut that they were supposed to defend against the onslaught of the opposing red team's attack. Debbie's team was also supposed to assault the red team's hut and she had volunteered to go with the rest of the attackers.

She could hear guns being fired all around her followed by the subsequent paint explosions on trees as well as people. She had watched people from both teams being hit and walking back to the safety zone to wait for the next game but she had remained safe behind her tree and waited for her chance. Debbie did not want to throw her 'life' away in this game before she had the opportunity to get her revenge on the slut Jennifer.

After what seemed an eternity the intensity of the battle subsided so Debbie decided to move forward to enter the fray. As she crawled forward she spotted a tall figure that looked female and who was a member of the red team. She was stand-

10

ing with her back to Debbie with no idea that she was in danger of being shot.

Debbie saw that the woman had auburn hair sticking out from the top of the mask which meant that this could only be the woman who had once tied her to her bed. Now the boot was on the other foot, for now she was at Debbie's mercy and she would now repay the woman for expecting her to lick pussy.

Suddenly Debbie felt the familiar excitement of having power over a helpless victim. With her gun in her hand she was in total control, a feeling that turned her on enormously, to the extent that she could feel her nipples already pushing against the fabric of her uniform. She detected that shameless pulse of arousal between her legs as she took aim and despatched a paintball in her prey's direction.

At that point the woman bent over in order to find some cover for herself but Debbie's paint pellet hit her smack on her left buttock. She stood up in total surprise only to be hit again as she turned to see where her assailant was hiding. Debbie's second shot landed square on the woman's right breast causing her to cry out at the sudden pain of the impact. In a desperate attempt to stop Debbie firing the woman put up her hands but Debbie was now possessed by the blood lust of battle. She continued to fire away at her target, catching the unfortunate woman with paint splats all over her body until she was covered in the bright yellow paint. Even though the woman started to scream that she had surrendered, Debbie continued to pelt her until her gun was almost emptied of balls.

Debbie's final shot caught the poor woman right between the tops of her thighs which meant that she bore the brunt of the painful blast directly on her sex. As the woman doubled up in agony Debbie laughed before plunging off into the undergrowth. Her pussy was now moist with excitement for she could feel the lining of her trousers sliding within the smooth

11

lips of her shaven sex to produce immensely satisfying sensations as she ran along. Even her tightly constrained breasts felt good as her hardened nipples rubbed ceaselessly against the rough material. This all made the long period of waiting in the midge ridden ditch behind the tree well worthwhile, especially when allied to the chance of doing the same thing to the hated Jennifer.

Debbie ran on thinking all the while of the things that she would do to Jennifer when she caught her.

The red team's hut came into sight ahead of her so she dropped down in the dirt to take stock. No one in sight, she crawled towards the hut in order to steal the glory and be the first to take the opposition's hut.

As she approached she heard a rustling behind her, the sun was shining through the trees but she could just make out a figure standing over her with a gun aimed straight at her head.

Debbie reacted by firing her gun at the person but she only heard a loud click as she pulled the trigger. She had used every single one of her fifty paint pellets to fire at the woman, and now was defenceless against the shadowy figure behind her.

In panic Debbie tried to get up but she soon felt the heel of a heavy boot in the small of her back forcing her back down to the ground with her masked face pressed in the mud.

"I think you're my prisoner now, you little tart," said a female voice that Debbie instantly recognised.

She groaned to herself, the person who had caught her was the very one that she herself had been seeking since the start of the game. It was Jennifer.

And so this was how she had come to be in the hands of her rival and she knew that this would be the dawn of a world of trouble for her. All at once her happiness evaporated and along with it any arousal that she might have felt. Now instead of being the powerful one, she was the prisoner under the control

12

of a woman she hated more than anybody else.

"Get up you slut and come with me," said the gleeful Jennifer. "You know the rules - I'm going to show you how we deal with blue team whores like you!"

With that Jennifer dragged Debbie to her feet by the tuft of dark hair that was sticking out of the top of her mask. Debbie turned to complain to her captor once she had stood up but her protestations were cut off with a nudge of Jennifer's gun in her back. Jennifer shoved her prisoner in the direction of a low valley beyond the main wood, triumphant in victory.

"And get your hands on your head like a proper prisoner of war," she said nastily once she had disarmed the fuming girl.

Debbie grudgingly placed her hands on her head before trudging off ahead of her triumphant captor. She thought of running away but she knew the rules which everybody had sworn to stick by neither did she want the penalties that would be imposed on her if she failed to comply. Besides that she was afraid that Jennifer would treat her in exactly the same way as Debbie had treted the other woman. The thought of all those paint splats across her body was too much to bear so she simply did as she was told, hoping that Jennifer too would play the game by the rules.

After ten minutes walking they came to the blue rope that the organisers had said they should not cross. Debbie stopped as she reached it but Jennifer insisted that they should cross the border to continue their trek. Debbie ducked reluctantly under the rope with the ever-vigilant Jennifer right behind her. Apparently the red team kept their prisoners outside the war zone, perhaps to keep them out of the main lines of fire. Debbie thought nothing more of it but simply carried on walking towards a small copse in the middle of the valley she had seen earlier. With every step she took she was aware that Jennifer was still there close behind her and plotting no doubt, as to what exactly she would do with her.

Debbie was relieved when they finally reached the trees for at least they had halted not that far away from the rest of the group and the battlefield. Jennifer would probably just hold her there until the next game to ensure that she did not rejoin the enemy.

However, Jennifer had an entirely different plan for Debbie which involved her being kept out of the game for the rest of the afternoon. She was absolutely delighted to have caught this strumpet so easily because it suited her purposes to have her at her mercy for so long.

"Spread yourself against that tree, you whore, so that I can check that you have no more weapons," said Jennifer in a most commanding voice.

Debbie decided that she would play along, even though it was obvious from her tight fitting suit that she simply couldn't hide a thing. She turned to face the nearest tree before leaning against it with her arms apart.

"Spread your legs, you bitch," shouted Jennifer kicking her victim's tightly clad legs apart with her booted foot.

"Alright, alright, whatever you say, boss," Debbie said spreading her legs to placate the zealous Jennifer.

"I didn't say you could talk, did I?" screeched Jennifer, furious at Debbie's sarcastic tone. "And get those damned legs apart before I make you!"

Debbie obeyed by pushing her legs as far apart as her trousers would allow. She was becoming a little disturbed by Jennifer's tone of voice but she still played along with the charade for fear of reprisals. She even pushed her pert bottom out in the hope that it would appeal to her captor.

Jennifer was pleased that Debbie seemed to be taking her captivity seriously at last for she was going to play her role of enemy interrogator to the full. The sight of Debbie's pert buttocks straining against her trousers told her that she was going to enjoy every minute of it.

She began to feel up the inside of Debbie's right leg whilst keeping her gun in her free hand. She traced the firm thigh muscles as she made her way up to the warm cleft at the top of her captive's legs.

Debbie jerked away as Jennifer's hand explored her, revolted by the prospect of this woman having such authority over her and gaining sexual pleasure from it. She had no choice but to allow this woman to continue her body search especially if she wanted to avoid breaking the rules.

Jennifer pushed her hand between Debbie's thighs in order to feel her mound through the fabric. She was astonished to find that the material was quite damp but decided not to comment about it at this stage in the proceedings. There would be plenty of time later to talk about this young woman's sexuality so she withdrew her hand in order to trace the curves of Debbie's voluptuous body. Slowly she moved her hand up the side of Debbie's quivering torso deviating from her path slightly to cup Debbie's left breast firmly in her hand.

Debbie could not believe that Jennifer was subjecting her to such close inspection or that her actions were turning her on so much. She moaned softly as Jennifer actually started to fondle her left nipple as part of her so-called search. Surely this wasn't allowed under the rules but whether she could or not Debbie found herself hoping that Jennifer would not stop.

However, Jennifer did stop because she heard a distant whistle signifying the end of that particular game. Quickly she grabbed one of Debbie's wrists so that she could snap a pair of handcuffs on her captive.

"What the hell..." spluttered Debbie.

"Shut it, bitch," spat Jennifer venomously. "You're staying out of the next game as well because of the shameless way you fell into my hands".

"But I..."

"Silence slut!" shouted Jennifer. "I am going to chain you to a tree so that I know where to find you when the next game starts!"

With that Jennifer dragged Debbie over to another slimmer tree so that she could pull her arms back around it. Another click of the free handcuff on Debbie's other wrist left her bound helplessly with her back to the trunk of the tree.

"Now you be a good little girl and stay there until I get back," Jennifer said with a patronising grin on her pretty face. "I haven't finished with you, in fact I have only just begun!"

"But you can't leave me like this..." cried Debbie but Jennifer was already sprinting back towards the blue rope in the distance.

Debbie pulled against the handcuffs but quickly realised that she had no choice but to remain exactly where she was, the shiny steel cuffs would not yield an inch. She sighed to herself for she really didn't want Jennifer to leave especially as she had aroused her so much with her wandering fingers.

She watched as Jennifer ran away hoping that it would not be too long until the lithe woman came back to finish what she had started. She could not understand it but this woman was certainly having an unexpected effect on her, an effect that turned her insides to jelly.

As she stood waiting in the midday heat Debbie wondered what Jennifer would do with her when she returned. She ached to touch her stiffened nipples but the handcuffs ensured that any more touching would have to be done by Jennifer. She even attempted to rub the tops of her thighs together to stimulate her clitoris but she couldn't seem to get the purchase she required.

Instead, she simply waited for Jennifer to return, passing

the time by imagining all the things that could be done to her in this helpless state of arousal. She thrust her breasts out as she pictured Jennifer squeezing her nipples again only this time much harder.

She saw herself sticking out her tongue to lick Jennifer's nipples whilst her captor encouraged her with a playful spank. She even thought that she would be prepared to lap at this woman's pussy even though she had flatly refused to do it when she had been at the mercy of the other woman.

Debbie could not believe the astonishing transformation in her feelings towards this woman to whom previously she wouldn't have given the time of day. Jennifer had taken control of her in the woods leading to the realisation for Debbie that this was exactly what she wanted. She wanted to be owned by a woman who could handle her as well as give her the thing she desperately wanted - sexual fulfilment. Jennifer it seemed could do both so Debbie waited with baited breath for her return.

Eventually she heard a faint whistle blast which was followed to her intense relief by the sight of Jennifer trotting across the field towards her. She was mesmerised by the way Jennifer's pert breasts bounced as she ran, confined within her hugging uniform.

"So you've decided to stay have you?" asked Jennifer sarcastically as she arrived at the tree.

"Yes, Miss," replied Debbie trying to get into the role of the submissive captive.

"Well, you'll be wishing that you'd managed to escape by the time I am through with you," said Jennifer bitchily.

She then proceeded to release one of Debbie's wrists only to rejoin them once she had pulled her away from the tree. When Debbie was secured again Jennifer produced a length of filthy rope which she loosely knotted around her prisoner's

17

neck leaving a piece dangling between her breasts as a make-shift leash.

Once she was sure that she had everything she needed with her including yet more rope, Jennifer lead her captive deeper into the wood.

Debbie of course had no choice but to follow, feeling thoroughly excited yet apprehensive about what would happen to her once they reached their destination.

After another ten minutes of walking away from the battle-field Jennifer selected what she decided was the perfect spot for Debbie's treatment. Ominously Debbie noticed that there were two trees about ten feet from each other which she was sure had something to do with Jennifer's choice.

"Kneel there, slut, while I get things ready," ordered Jennifer brusquely.

"Yes, Miss," Debbie responded falling to her knees instantly.

Jennifer took more pieces of rope out of the thigh pockets of her combat trousers and tied a length to each of Debbie's wrists. She then pulled her quarry back between the designated trees and made her stand with her head bowed in submission.

Jennifer quickly undid one of the cuffs before pulling the roped wrist out towards the tree to her left. She secured the other end of the rope to the trunk a few feet higher than Debbie's head then repeated the process with her right wrist. This left Debbie standing in the small clearing with her arms bound uselessly above her. She was completely helpless but at least she was still clothed for to be naked in this position would have been extremely unnerving.

It came as a shock therefore when Jennifer booted her legs apart again before bending over to tie lengths of rope to each of Debbie's ankles. In a moment Jennifer had her ankles tied and stretched apart to both tree trunks which made Debbie even

18

more vulnerable.

At this point both girls heard the distant sound of the whistle so Jennifer turned to run from her tethered victim. Debbie glared at her retreating captor wondering how she could possibly leave her trussed up like this so far from civilisation.

"Please don't leave me, Miss," she begged but to no avail for Jennifer carried on running.

Not wanting to be left in this way Debbie began to scream as loudly as she could. This had the desired effect for Jennifer stopped in her tracks and started back towards the clearing pulling something of a whitish colour out of yet another pocket as she did so.

"I didn't want to have to do this just yet, but you have clearly forced my hand!" said Jennifer sternly. "Now get your mouth open you little slut while I silence you."

Debbie reluctantly opened her mouth as Jennifer pulled her mask up from her hot, sweaty face. Deftly she pushed the white material into Debbie's mouth forcing it in as deep as she could with her fingers.

Debbie gagged as the fabric touched the back of her throat but Jennifer sealed her mouth with masking tape before her prisoner could push it out with her tongue. When she was satisfied that Debbie had been hushed Jennifer pulled the girl's mask back down over her face before walking off to rejoin the battle.

Debbie watched her go, resigned to the fact that she would have to remain tied between the two trees until her captor decided to return. She certainly could no longer call for assistance for Jennifer's gag was effective indeed at keeping her quiet.

The material that packed her mouth felt silky and tasted like nothing Debbie had come across before. It reminded her of the time when she had been ordered to lick another woman's

19

pussy that time on the bed. Only the smell of the dominatrix's moist vulva remained in her memory from that encounter for she had refused to lap at the gaping sex thrust in her face. But it was a taste and smell similar to the aroma she had detected as she was being gagged by Jennifer.

With a start Debbie realised what her gag was made of as well as what her captor had done before silencing her. The material in her mouth was obviously Jennifer's panties which she had made sure were wet with her own juices before shoving them into Debbie's mouth.

The bitter sweet flavour of Jennifer's arousal now filled her mouth throwing her feelings into total confusion. Previously the thought of tasting another woman had completely revolted her but now she was rather turned on by the idea.

Ironically the fact that it was the hated Jennifer's pussy juices that she was being made to savour made her subjection even sweeter. This made the degradation of her current circumstances even more acute, which in turn fuelled her inexplicable arousal. She had no choice but to obey her captor which meant that she was now somehow justified in being turned on by her plight.

As she waited for Jennifer to come back to her Debbie began to think of all the things she might be subjected to by her new mistress. She realised that she certainly could not resist Jennifer and this aroused her even more as she pulled uselessly against her bonds.

The distant sounds of the raging battle were lost to Debbie as she pondered Jennifer's return. She hoped that Jennifer would allow her to relieve what was becoming an overwhelming tingling sensation between her legs. She knew that her pussy was wet for she had detected a tiny trickle of her juices as it snaked its way down her upper thigh. She could also feel her nipples as they hardened against her combat suit, once again confirming that she was actually enjoying being tied spread-eagled in

20

the open air.

The plastic visor of her mask steamed up as she imagined Jennifer massaging her breasts and pinching her nipples to her heart's content. Debbie closed her eyes so she could picture more clearly the moment when her captor allowed her to come for the first time. Her breathing quickened as she tried to rub her pussy against her trousers once more. She pushed her hips forward but was unable to reach the rough seams with her swollen clit, which left her more frustrated as well as unfulfilled.

In her efforts to gain some satisfaction she failed to notice that the battle had ceased again or that Jennifer was making her way back to her as quickly as she could.

As she arrived at the clearing she could see Debbie struggling against her bonds but she realised immediately that she was not trying to escape but that she was attempting to pleasure herself. The girl was desperate to come but there was no way that she could without a little help from her mistress.

Jennifer smiled to herself at the ease with which she was turning this slut around. It would not be long before she reduced this haughty bitch to a drivelling slave ready to obey her every command. She would also be more willing to comply with the demands of her colleagues who had told Jennifer about the way Debbie had used and then snubbed them all over the last couple of years.

But then this was what the whole paintballing trip had been about. It was simply an elaborate way for Jennifer to gain revenge on Debbie on behalf of the rest of the office staff who had suffered because of her bitchiness to them. Her capture had all been planned in advance and the rest of the staff knew exactly where Debbie was as well as what was being done to her.

Maybe later on Jennifer would allow some of the others to

come and gaze upon this specimen that she was going to tame, though for the moment she was hers to play with alone. She would make this bitch beg for an orgasm before she was through with her but first she would administer the well-earned punishment.

"So you're trying to play with yourself are you, you little whore?" Jennifer whispered into her squirming prisoner's ear.

Debbie jumped for she thought that she was still alone in the throes of her passion. She was acutely embarrassed to have been discovered in her state of arousal by her captor but it was also deliciously naughty to be caught in the act of trying to reach orgasm.

"Well we have ways of dealing with disgraceful sluts like you," said Jennifer menacingly. "And one of the ways is with this gun!"

Debbie wondered what on earth she meant with that threat for she had hoped that she would be chastised for masturbating with a whip of some sort. The gun seemed a lame sort of punishment at first until she remembered how it had felt to be shot with one of the paint pellets at close range. She recalled how much Jennifer's paint ball had hurt her as she had squirmed on the ground under her boot. She also thought about the way she had made that woman dance in pain by emptying her cartridge of pellets over her helplessly writhing body.

Debbie shuddered for at least the woman had had the chance to dodge some of her shots. Tied between the trees as she was Debbie would have no choice but to stand and take everything Jennifer wanted to give her.

She watched through the haze of her steamed up mask as Jennifer walked around behind her to take up her stance with her gun at her side. Debbie tried to plead with her to make her change her mind but Jennifer's panties stuffed in her mouth ensured that the only sound she could make was a muffled squawk.

Jennifer steadied herself before taking aim about ten feet from her victim. She examined the bright yellow burst of her first shot when she had captured Debbie which had dried in the shape of some strange wild flower. There would be a fair few more of them before Jennifer was finished with her.

Without any warning Jennifer pulled the trigger to release the first paintball which impacted on Debbie's right buttock with a satisfying splat.

Debbie screamed into her gag as she struggled to cope with the sudden pain that exploded across her bottom. She had been expecting Jennifer to fire her gun but the shot still came as a nasty shock to her, it seemed just as agonising as the initial shot when Jennifer had first caught her.

Happy with her first attempt Jennifer fired a second time high up on Debbie's left thigh. This produced a similar strangled cry from her victim as well as another pretty yellow pattern on the canvas of her combat pants.

Jennifer's third shot evened up the other three paint marks as it caught Debbie high up on the back of her upper right thigh causing her to jolt forward in agony once again. She screamed for mercy as loudly as she could into her gag but her words were lost in the damp material of her tormentor's panties.

Debbie yanked on the ropes that held her between the trees but Jennifer's knots did not give an inch for it seemed that she was an expert at securing her prey. There was no way Debbie could escape from her bonds so she had no choice but to stand in front of Jennifer's gun with no protection for her body save her thin uniform.

Letting her head fall forward Debbie resigned herself to suffer as many of the formidable paintballs as Jennifer cared to unleash upon her helpless frame. At least the combat trousers took some of the sting of the pellets for it would have been dreadful to be shot at with nothing on.

Debbie shivered with fear as she thought of being naked before this woman's gun but her dread was tinged with excitement at the possibility of being stripped by her captor. As the pellets continued to burst excruciatingly upon her buttocks Debbie delighted in the thought of squirming in her captivity with absolutely nothing on.

Despite the build-up of pain from the impact of the pellets Debbie found herself being aroused by her fantasies. These disturbing ideas were actually further fuelled by the increasing discomfort of her position and left her stimulated beyond her control.

She pulled on the ropes with all her might, so desperate was she to free herself in order to fulfil the carnal desires deep within her. She wanted to rip off her clothes so that she could feel her excited body with hands that were keen to pinch her nipples or even stroke her own pussy.

Once more Debbie closed her eyes against the pain of the bright yellow barrage upon her constrained torso to concentrate her mind on the images in her head. Pictures of her naked body swam before her eyes with the dominating presence of Jennifer never far away, ready to bring her pain or pleasure at her own volition.

Debbie thrust her hips forward again in a futile attempt to gain satisfaction. She no longer cared about what Jennifer would think of her for she was only a helpless hostage tortured by her kidnapper as well as her own base cravings.

It was not her fault that she was in this dilemma so she felt justified in behaving in this obviously wanton way. She swayed her hips with total abandon in search of fulfilment but pleasure was denied to her because of the cruel way in which Jennifer had spread her legs between the tree trunks. Her all-consuming quest for gratification led her off into a little world of her own, to the extent that she did not even notice when the volley had stopped. So lost was she in the haze of her journey of self-discovery that she did not realise that Jennifer was standing right in front of her until she spoke.

"So you're at it again are you, you naughty little tart," said Jennifer not unpleasantly. "Well it's time for me to go back to the battle now but I will leave you a little something to set you thinking before I go."

With that Jennifer detached a large knife from her belt it had a six inch blade attached to an even longer handle. Debbie saw through her misty goggles that its sharp edge glinted in the sunlight which made her nervous indeed as to Jennifer's intentions for her. She was now terrified of her captor for she could do anything she wanted to her, anything at all.

"I won't be needing this until a little later so you can look after it for me, can't you?" enquired Jennifer even though Debbie could not reply.

Jennifer unfastened the buttons on the front of Debbie's trousers before yanking them down a short way over her hips.

"My, these are a tight fit, aren't they my dear?" she asked mischievously.

She knew full well that the trousers were too tight for Debbie because she had chosen them especially for her prisoner prior to the first battle. Jennifer had wanted to watch her struggle into them before hobbling off to war in her over- sized boots that had also been chosen by her.

Jennifer pulled down the front of Debbie's trousers a little more before inserting the knife into the gap, handle first. She made sure that the end of the handle was securely wedged between Debbie's labia which were moist with her oozing juices.

"Well, we are a very turned on little slut, aren't we?" Jennifer said delighted at the effect she was having on her hostage.

When she was satisfied that the knife was in the just the

right place for maximum effect she patted her victim's right buttock. With a sly wink she ran off towards the sound of the developing battle leaving Debbie straining between the two trees.

Debbie was still desperate to play with herself but at least Jennifer had created an interesting possibility for her this time. The handle of the knife was nestled between her dripping lips above, her swollen clitoris pressed down on the guard of the handle which meant that even though she was still bound she could at least pleasure herself.

She began to push her hips forward in order to rub her hardening bud against the rubber of the handle which was quickly lubricated by her sodden pussy. Tiny shivers of excitement jolted up her spine as she increased the force of her pelvic thrusts.

It was not long before she was steaming up the visor of her mask again with short passionate breaths. She sucked on the panties in her mouth as she neared her first orgasm which churned in her stomach like a whirlpool.

Debbie could not believe that she had been driven to behave in this outrageous way by a woman that she detested but she could not help herself. She had no choice but to ride the knife that Jennifer had left there to taunt her so that she could relieve at least some of her pent-up frustrations.

When she finally came she yelled as loudly as she could into her gag not caring for a moment whether anybody was there to hear her complete surrender to her animal cravings. Debbie had been building up to that moment of ultimate satisfaction ever since she had squeezed her self into her uniform so she enjoyed every second of her wild abandonment.

With her eyes tightly closed once again Debbie could see a myriad of stars darting through the black void as she travelled to her own personal heaven. Feelings so good just didn't come any better than this even though it was due mainly to the ministrations of her hated rival. Perhaps she had misjudged this woman after all for she certainly knew how to make a girl enjoy herself.

However, this illusion of a benevolent dictator was completely shattered when Debbie opened her eyes for before her stood the grinning Jennifer. She had obviously sneaked back to observe her captive as she twisted between the trees in the throes of her shattering orgasm. A wave of embarrassment drowned the passion that had risen within the writhing Debbie who was now mortified with shame. Someone had seen her seen experiencing her orgasm after all and to make it worse it was the woman who had forced her to degrade herself in the first place.

"I knew that you would enjoy the knife handle if I put it there," Jennifer said happily. "I simply couldn't resist hanging around to see what you would do with it and you certainly didn't disappoint me, did you?"

Debbie hung her head in humiliation for she had been totally broken by the woman she now regarded as her mistress. Any fight that she had left had been drained from her during the course of her crushing climax. All she could do was hang limply in her bonds as Jennifer prepared to torment her once again.

She watched through the semi-misted visor as Jennifer approached her with a huge smile still splitting her beautiful face. Debbie was annoyed that Jennifer was enjoying torturing her so much but there was absolutely nothing that she could do about it stretched so tightly as she was.

"Well, I think that I will use this knife in a more conventional way, if you don't mind," said Jennifer as she pulled the makeshift probe from Debbie's trousers. "But first let's see what you taste like, you naughty little girl."

27

Debbie could not believe it as she saw Jennifer lift the knife handle to her mouth before licking along its slippery length with her tongue. This heightened Debbie's mortification because it was obvious that Jennifer was relishing the fruits of her labours as she savoured the very essence of her helpless plaything.

"Very nice, I must say and I wonder if you've ever tasted yourself," said Jennifer appreciably. "I bet you have you slut and there will be plenty of time to find out when I have finished with you here but let's see a little more of you first!"

With that Jennifer wiped the handle on her sleeve then advanced menacingly on the quivering Debbie who tried in vain to pull away from her. The sun glinted on the blade as Jennifer seized Debbie's camouflaged top with her free hand before slashing away at the material with the sharp serrated edge.

Debbie gasped as Jennifer systematically cut away the seams of her combat jacket until it fell in a useless heap at her feet leaving her full breasts to spill out free.

Jennifer paused in her efforts to admire Debbie's ripe nipples, which she thought would look even better if adorned with a pair of crocodile clips. She made a mental note to retrieve those painful little items on her next visit to her car when the current battle had finished.

Next she turned her attention to Debbie's trousers, which she dispatched with a few deft strokes of her knife leaving Debbie helplessly naked before her tormentor.

"You've got a good body, girl, I'll give you that," said Jennifer flatteringly as she surveyed the cruelly spread Debbie's charms. "But I'm going to make you regret the way you've been flirting with it around the office."

From Debbie's heavy breasts Jennifer let her eyes rove down over her flat stomach to her pussy. She leisurely examined her

28

shaven sex, which was still dripping with her juices, admiring the way her lips pouted between her creamy white thighs. She certainly felt fortunate to have such a specimen at her mercy but she had made a promise that she fully intended to fulfil before their day together was over.

"I'm going to go again now because I have to fetch a few things," announced Jennifer airily. "I'm also going to bring a friend of mine along. In fact I think you might know her, because she's the one whose pussy you refused to lick. She might have something to say about that when she arrives!"

Debbie looked on horror as her tormentor turned to walk away for she thought that her humiliation was for Jennifer's eyes only. She had not expected to be left on display in front of anyone else, least of all the woman who she had so rudely rejected in her own bedroom.

Frantically she tugged at the ropes in an attempt to free herself only to be reminded that she would remain bound between her trees until Jennifer saw fit to release her. All she could do was wait for Jennifer and her friend to return; her friend who was soon to see her trust up naked like a pagan sacrifice.

In the distance she could hear the sounds of the battle with the ceaseless popping of the compressed air guns. As long as the fighting went on she knew that she would be safe but the sound of the whistle would herald the return of her captor only this time with her colleague.

Sure enough, soon after the latest battle had ceased Debbie saw two camouflaged figures making their way through the woods towards her. Debbie gulped as she saw that one of them was carrying a rucksack no doubt filled with more things to torture her with. Even more ominous was the fact that one of them was covered from head to toe with the tell-tale florets of paintball impacts.

They both had their masks on their faces but Debbie noticed that they were both laughing merrily as they approached her. They were both intent on having a great deal of fun with her before the day was through which meant that Debbie had a lot more suffering to endure before her ordeal was over.

"So this is what you've done with the whore, is it?" asked the taller of the two women as she took off her mask.

Debbie cringed as she saw that it was indeed the woman who she had refused to serve, and who she had pelted with paintballs earlier in the day. Her distinctive auburn hair fell to her shoulders as the woman removed the straps from the back of her head, reminding Debbie of just how attractive she was and why she had agreed to go out with her in the first place.

"Well, pretty one, I think that we have some unfinished business, don't we?" said the woman menacingly as she stroked Debbie's defenceless breast with the back of her gloved hand.

"Oh, yes, Marcia and don't forget that it was this one who emptied her cartridge at you after you'd surrendered!" offered Jennifer enthusiastically as she too removed her mask.

"So it was this bitch that covered me with bruises was it?" exclaimed the outraged woman checking her that her gun had enough pellets in it for revenge. "At least I have the chance to get my own back and I am sure that these things hurt much more on naked flesh, you cow!"

Debbie desperately tried to pull away from the woman who was about to visit her with more pain than she could possibly bear. She was about to fire her remaining paint balls at her exposed form point blank but there was nothing that Debbie could do to stop her.

As Marcia walked round behind the struggling Debbie she drank in the sight of her slender body squirming in her inescapable bondage. She had fancied this girl ever since tempting her to come back to her flat but now she really did have her at her mercy.

She loved the way Debbie's flat stomach heaved as she fought against the ropes as well as the swell of her breasts when she sucked in air through her mask. She would have great fun teaching this slut a lesson with the ingenious new method of chastising that Jennifer seemed to have invented.

Marcia took aim with her compressed air-powered paintball gun; she had the base Debbie's spine in her sights and lowered the gun so that she could launch her first shot between her victim's buttocks.

Debbie heard the loud pop of the gun a fraction of a second before the wretched paintball exploded across the flesh of her naked cheeks. She screamed in agony for it was much worse without the protection of the combat trousers. Debbie could almost feel the first bruise forming under the quickly drying paint over her buttocks.

Marcia's second shot burst across her cheeks with a force that threw Debbie's hips towards the watching Jennifer who smiled wickedly at her victim's predicament.

A third pellet hit Debbie agonisingly between her buttocks to cause her body once more to dance forward within the tight restrictions of her bonds.

"I could stand and watch this all day," exclaimed Jennifer. "But I think it's time to get some pictures of this little bitch, don't you?"

"Yes, but what's wrong with keeping the slut like this?" asked Marcia, disappointed that she had been made to stop her cannonade.

"Well, I'll take a couple like this as you fire some more of your pellets at her cute backside," said Jennifer. "However, I want to try her in one more position before we make her do what she wouldn't do for you before."

"Sounds great to me, " replied Marcia, joyfully taking aim

with her gun as Jennifer produced an expensive looking camera from her bag.

Debbie moaned into her gag whilst she helplessly watched the two women preparing their impromptu photo shoot. She thought that she had been humiliated enough by them but to have evidence of her disgrace on film was even more shaming.

Debbie let her head drop forward in total defeat for she guessed that they would use these pictures of her somehow long after her ordeal was over. She did not put it past these women to want to keep some sort of hold over her even after they released her from her current bonds. However, her thoughts of future suffering were interrupted by the very present torment she was enduring as the report of the gun combined with the click of Jennifer's camera preceded yet another barrage of agony over her aching bottom. Even behind the mask and the gag Debbie's tortured expression told the story of her anguish which Jennifer committed to celluloid with every eagerly taken snapshot.

"Let's get a couple of pictures of your paintballs hitting her breasts," suggested Jennifer, beckoning Marcia to go round to Debbie's front for better effect.

Debbie desperately tried to beg the pair not to carry out this part of their plan but to no avail for she could see Marcia trotting round in front of her to take up her new position.

"Make sure you hit her on her nipples because I want to get a shot of the paint squashing her breasts," said Jennifer enthusiastically.

Debbie tried to steady her trembling as both women took aim but as they depressed their triggers she began to shake with fear. She knew that this impact would hurt more than the rest and she was not wrong.

Jennifer laughed as the paint smeared itself in a pretty pattern on Debbie's left breast which was briefly pushed in like a crushed egg shell. As her spongy flesh juddered back into shape some of the liquid paint fell onto her leg leaving a luminescent dribble on her thigh.

"This is great stuff," cried Jennifer over Debbie's groans. "I know a man who will pay a fortune for these if the little tart doesn't do exactly as she's told when we let her go!"

Poor Debbie only vaguely heard the threat as she floundered in her own sea of pain for the sensitive flesh of her breast still tingled with the aftershocks of the assault upon it. She did not know how much more of this treatment she could stand before she passed out but it was clear that she was at the mercy of two very experienced torturers.

Debbie tried to flinch away as she saw Marcia lining up her next shot but the unyielding ropes ensured that she was still in place as the next pellet caught her full on her right breast. She jerked in her bonds before yelling hopelessly into her gag as she was engulfed in yet more pain from her paint-splattered nipples.

"Fantastic!" shouted Jennifer. "Now for the one she's been waiting for - between her legs, the little whore!"

Debbie gulped back her tears as she realised what Jennifer had in store for her. So far the paintballs had landed only on the fleshy parts of her defenceless body but this last shot was to be directed towards the most sensitive part of her body of all, namely her pussy.

She trembled as she watched Marcia lift her gun one more time with the sights set firmly at her exposed and gaping sex which would take the full impact of this latest blow. Once again she tried to beg for mercy but all in vain for Marcia simply pulled the trigger to release another stinging paintball.

The moment the pellet hit her Debbie was transported to yet another level of agony for her vulva was ignited into an orgy of fiery torment. She did not realise that pain like this existed but it hit her like a fist in the stomach before she thankfully passed out.

When she finally came round she was aware of a constant nagging ache in her wrists and shoulders as well as the throb of the pain between her legs. She looked up to investigate the source of the new discomfort only to realise that she had been moved whilst she had been unconscious.

She now found herself hanging from a sturdy branch of another tree by a length of rope which was wrapped around her wrists. Her feet were now bound tightly together but dangled uselessly above the ground forcing her entire weight onto her burning wrists.

"Ah, welcome back," said a voice nastily. "We wondered when you would grace us with your presence again!"

Debbie looked to her side to see Jennifer standing there with her camera ready to record the next stage of her chastisement. She could not see the dreaded Marcia but Debbie guessed that she would not be too far away for she would not want to miss whatever Jennifer had in store for her.

In fact it was Marcia who startled Debbie as she prodded her in the middle of her back with her gun.

"Yes, we want to put you into a spin, so to speak," laughed Marcia. "And we would hate for you to miss it!"

Debbie wondered what on earth the sadistic bitch meant, but she did not have to think about it too long as she saw Marcia taking aim with her gun once more.

Another loud pop followed by the impact of a painful paint splat on her upper thigh twisted Debbie violently to her left. Debbie felt herself careering out of control as the force of the shot spun her around to face the opposite direction where Jennifer was waiting with her gun.

Jennifer fired immediately but this time the pellet caught

Debbie on her left thigh which propelled her back in the opposite direction towards the waiting Marcia. Debbie screamed
pitifully into her gag knowing that she was just their plaything
and that this new sport could go on for a very long time or at
least as long as they had pellets.

"This is great!" exclaimed Marcia. "It's just like the swing-
ball game I used to play as a kid only with paint guns instead of
bats."

"I knew you would like it," replied Jennifer happily. "Now
I must get some shots of this before we cut her down and set
her to work."

As the camera flashed and whirred again Debbie knew
that she was already practically owned by these two bitches.
She realised that she would do almost anything to prevent the
others in the office seeing these pictures. She was completely
trapped and the pictures would ensure that her indenture to
these woman would last just as long as they wanted it to.

Debbie began to go dizzy as she span round because of the
accumulation of pain with every fresh application of paint.
The woods went past her eyes in a blur and she felt herself
blacking out once more as she struggled to take in the consequences of her capture.

But the merciful release from her suffering did not last long
for Jennifer brought her round slapping her face with the back
of her hand.

She realised that she was no longer strung up from the tree
but that she was lying on the ground at the feet of her two
captors. Her hands were tied behind her back with the coarse
rope and she could see clearly now for her mask had been
removed.

The panties however, were still stuffed securely in her mouth
so it was clear that she was not meant to make any sound.
Debbie looked around to discover where her tormentors were

so she could plead somehow for release, but she could not see them.

"Here we are, darling," said a voice above her. "And we have a couple of little jobs for you to do for us!"

Debbie looked up to see that Marcia was sitting on a branch over her head whilst her partner-in-crime climbed up to take her place next to her. They were both naked except for their army boots with their long legs spread obscenely wide ready for action.

Even though the thought of it revolted her Debbie knew exactly what they wanted her to do but she was not about to disobey the woman now. Her body ached all over, especially where the paint had already hardened across her skin so she was keen not to incur any more punishment from them.

She struggled to get to her knees so that she could work her way over to a spot below the women where she could more easily carry our her allotted task. Debbie would have to stand so that she could bend forward between the women's legs but she was concerned that she could not do her job properly with her gag in place.

"Get yourself between Marcia's legs first, as she is the one who you so cruelly rejected before," ordered Jennifer.

Debbie obeyed as quickly as she could, climbing to her feet between the thighs of the stern looking Marcia. She could see pearls of dew forming on Marcia's labia which were poking out through her shortly cropped pubic hair.

"Now you, little bitch," said Marcia wickedly. "Are you ready to continue where you so rudely left off?"

Debbie nodded her head vigorously, hoping that this reaction would earn her a reprieve from further paintballing.

"And would you like me to take those tiny wet panties out of your mouth so that you can serve me properly this time?"

Again Debbie showed her acquiescence as enthusiastically

as she could under the circumstances.

"Very well, let's see you prove yourself to us," said Marcia as she removed the tape and the panties. "But woe betide you of you fail to satisfy us completely with that tongue of yours, do you hear?"

Fearing further repercussions if she spoke Debbie nodded her head before dipping her lips forward towards Marcia's gaping sex. She wrinkled her nose up when she smelt the strong aroma of Marcia's arousal but she simply had no choice but to stick out her tongue in order to lick between the sodden pussy lips.

To her surprise Debbie found that the taste wasn't that bad after all, not unlike her own which she had experienced many times when she had masturbated alone in her room.

Perhaps these two would prove to be good tormentors in the future, just so long as they weren't too free with their paintballs...

Looking down at the black riding crop sticking out of the leather boots of the female soldier in front of me I realised that I was in bigger trouble than I had at first thought. Even though she was a woman it was clear that she was delighted to have us in her clutches so I began to fear what she intended to do with the pair of us.

It had been a long reconnaissance flight and I had not been concentrating properly for I ended up getting myself and my observer shot down over Stalingrad on the wrong side of the river Volga.

Our Messerschmidt 110 had been hit by flak over the eastern part of the city and had gone down in a flurry of flames, but Karl and I had managed to bail out just in time to avoid an untimely death in the doomed crate.

1However, as we gathered up our parachutes in an effort to hide them away we knew that we were in trouble when a Russian patrol of about a dozen soldiers in brown uniforms headed our way over the wasteland. Someone had seen our slow descent to earth and they were after us. Because there seemed no chance of escaping without being shot we had put up our hands and hoped for the best, although there wasn't really much hope of kind treatment by any member of the Russian army or public for that matter.

As the troops approached us we noticed that they didn't look like ordinary Russian soldiers, not that we had seen many from our vantage point high above the Steppes. We knew that the ground troops hated us fly boys but now we were going to find out just how much they loathed us.

But these soldiers did look different and as they came closer we realised why - they were all women; the women that Stalin had sent against us with their menfolk; the women that were

38

just as thirsty for revenge against the Germans as the men, if not more so.

And so it was into the tender mercies of the women of the 103rd Rifle Division that we were taken on that bright December afternoon of 1942 with no hope of release or repatriation until they had dealt with the pair of us in their own special way.

"What is your name and what was your mission?" shouted a tall slender woman with a shock of blonde hair framing a hard but attractive face. She was evidently the leader of the patrol.

"Captain Wilhelm Schneider of the German Luftwaffe, number 357621," I replied with as much dignity as I could muster under the circumstances. "And this is Sergeant Karl Muller, number 629834."

"You will address me as 'Miss' from now on, do you understand me, you German scum?" demanded the blonde who stared straight at me with her piercing blue eyes.

"But I object.... ..." I stammered.

"You gave up your rights to object to anything the moment your army invaded mother Russia," snapped the woman. "And before we hand you over to our authorities my girls and I are going to exact our own revenge for the way you bastards destroyed our cities!"

That confirmed for me that we were in for a hard time with these women for they seemed hell-bent on extracting payment for the sins of the German army from our sorry hides. We were indeed unfortunate to have floated down into their territory.

"Tie them up and bring them back to our base," she ordered. "We'll soon make them sorry that they ever messed with us Ruskies."

With that, four of her troopers ran forward in order to bind our wrists behind our backs with oily rope that they had picked up from the floor. My wrists burnt instantly as one of the women

39

zealously pulled the ropes around them as tightly as she could before securing them with an even tighter knot.

Once they were happy that we were securely bound they threw ropes around our necks and dragged us off towards their camp, which turned out be in a disused factory near the Volga. It was a damp smelly place with a hole in the roof where the tiles had come loose with the only light coming from candles set upon tables around the walls.

There were many other women in the large room in various states of undress for we had obviously arrived at the time of their ablutions. Mud-spattered uniforms lay in untidy piles around the floor as some of the women gathered round a tub of water to bathe themselves.

I could not help but admire the nubile young soldiers as they washed themselves, completely unconcerned at our appearance amongst them. They laughed with one another as they frolicked with the water, their breasts bouncing free of any material fetters.

"So you like to look at my girls do you, you fascist swine?" inquired the woman scornfully. "It's pretty little things like this that you have been bombing night after night!"

"But we are only reconnaissance fliers..." stammered Karl.

"You will not speak without permission," interrupted the blonde. "It is obvious that I will have to teach you how to behave. Tanya! Bring the special gags for me!"

"Yes, Captain," said a petite girl with long auburn hair and gorgeous brown eyes.

Whilst I watched the girl scamper off to retrieve the mysterious gags I considered the idea of myself and our captor being officers - captains. I considered the possibility that she would let me go but these hopes were dashed as the girl returned with a canvas bag in her hand.

"Now you heroes of the Luftwaffe, you're going to taste

something that you've probably never tasted before but I recommend it, because it is a taste that you will become very familiar with," said the Russian captain menacingly.

At a click of her fingers four of her girls grabbed us whilst another two pulled various pieces of white material out of the bag.

"We don't get much chance to wash these as we are busy girls," continued the captain with a mischievous smile on her face. "So I think that you will appreciate why they smell and taste the way they do!"

With that the girls held the pungent fabric against our clenched teeth so that our nostrils were filled with the flavour of most of the girls in the company. Sweat mingled with pussy juices and other bodily secretions in a heady mix that overwhelmed my senses but somehow stimulated me at the same time. Perhaps it was the sight of all those firm young breasts around the rain barrel combined with the thought that the undergarments stuffed against my mouth had been next to their juicy pussies. I couldn't believe that these thoughts were taking over my mind even as I opened my mouth and two of the soldiers fixed the gags in place with surgical tape. I found myself having to concentrate on the dangerousness of our situation in order to avoid having an embarrassing erection there and then in front of all those girls. I tried to think about how I was going to escape but my mind swam with all the possibilities that being held captive by these girls threw up.

"Now take them away, I will deal with them later," commanded the blonde captain. "And bring me the one who tried to escape, it is high time I punished him for his clumsy attempt to evade us!"

A shiver ran down my spine as two young women led us away from the soldier's recreation room for I wondered what she was going to do to the escapee.

I also began to reconsider my feeble plan to escape because I feared the consequences if I or Karl failed to get away. Instead I meekly followed the young lady who dragged me down a long dark corridor towards an unknown fate.

She had short dark hair which fell in a bob above the shoulders of her close-fitting brown tunic, which was what most of the women seemed to be wearing. Her tight pants were tucked into black leather boots like those of her captain but I noted with a certain relief that she did not carry a whip.

As I watched her cute bottom swaying from side to side under the taut fabric I pictured her pretty face with her grey eyes and her pouting lips. I felt that this girl would not let us come to any harm wherever she was taking us, for she was far too beautiful to be cruel.

My pleasant thoughts about the girl evaporated as soon as she opened the door of what was to become our cell. What I saw in the large dark room shocked me to the core because there we several naked men in the chamber in various states of confinement and obvious distress.

As I looked round the dingy room I saw two men in cages and two men chained up behind bars in tiny cubicles along the far wall and all were gagged in a similar way to Karl and myself. In addition to this a man was hanging by his wrists above the floor with his toes vainly searching for support for his stretched body.

The men in the cages were doubled over with their wrists tied behind their backs with some sort of wire. Their heads were thrust down between their knees whilst their flesh bulged through the small squares of the metal that encased them. But that was by no means the worst for under their cages I noticed that their testicles and their penises had been forced through a small hole and bound with yet more wire around the bases of their flaccid cocks.

To make matters worse both cages had been suspended by rope above small tables upon which were placed candles that burnt directly below their bound scrotums. The flames seemed at times to briefly touch the tips of their penises, which made the already moaning men groan louder in the agony of torment.

I dreaded to think what they had done to receive such brutal treatment, but once again we were drawn away from the scene towards a couple of heavy wooden boxes in the corner, which were punctured with tiny air holes for the intended inhabitants.

It appeared that these were to be our homes for a while for our warders forced us to climb, still trussed up tightly, into the chests before locking the lids shut over our heads. I could hardly breathe because I was folded away neatly like a blanket but at least I could see out through one of the little holes.

From the cramped confines of the box I watched the man hanging in the centre of the room who seemed to the two girls' next target. They walked over to him speaking Russian in their husky voices, obviously taunting him about what was to happen to him next.

They cut the rope with a bayonet thus allowing him to fall to the ground in a crumpled heap at their feet. Without allowing him any time to recover they pulled him back up so that they could haul him out of the room to what no doubt would be further excruciating punishment.

Once they had gone I could do nothing but contemplate my fate which was exacerbated by the fact that I could hear both caged men wailing into their gags piteously as the candles burned under their helpless genitalia.

I wondered how long it might be before I too would be screaming my head off under that sort of treatment. Beyond the groaning coming from the dangling cages I could soon hear distant screams, which I presumed were emanating from the man who had been taken from the room earlier. Each cry was preceded by a faint cracking sound that made my blood run cold.

In an attempt to take my mind off the crazy world into which I had parachuted I tried to make myself as comfortable as I could in my box. This was by no means easy for there was no spare room at all and my joints had started aching almost as soon as the lid had been jammed shut.

All I could do was resign myself to wait for whatever was going to happen whilst not thinking too hard about the strange cacophony of tortured sounds that I could hear from all over the factory.

After what seemed like an age the two girls brought the man back into the room with his buttocks and his back covered with vivid red whip marks. They threw him to the floor before dragging him by his hair over to one of the cells in the wall.

As the girls padlocked the man's cell the dark haired one glanced over to the box in which I was cowering. She was sweating from the exertion of dealing with the poor tormented man but she looked keen to start whatever torture the captain had in store for me.

"Time to get the flyboy captain out for madam to play with," she laughed to her comrade. "I think that she has something really special in store for him."

With that the girls came over to my box and released the lid above me. I was pleased to be able to breathe properly again as they dragged me out but I was worried about what the 'something special' was. My Russian was poor but the meaning was clear.

Once again they produced the terrifying bayonet which they used to cut away my attire piece by piece. They were not satisfied until every shred of my blue Luftwaffe uniform was lying in a heap on the floor leaving me stark naked in front of these unnerving females. They spoke now in broken German, not good but understandable.

"Not a bad cock for the invading vermin," said the dark haired girl.

"Yes, we can have some fun with that when the captain has finished with him," replied her friend enthusiastically.

I did not like the sound of any of that at all but I had no choice but to comply with their wishes as once more I was hauled out of the room by a short rope slung around my neck. They rushed me along the corridor quicker this time but their delightfully wiggling bottoms held no comfort for me as I approached my impending doom.

As I re-entered the main recreation room I was embarrassed to note that most of the girls were fully dressed in their combat uniforms. Some had their guns slung over their shoulders as if ready for patrols but it was clear that they were going to observe at least some of what was going to happen to my naked form before they left.

"Ah, the gallant pilot back from his trip to the holding cells; do you like your new accommodation?" asked the captain sarcastically. "Of course, I forgot, he still has the taste of Soviet pussy in his mouth - Tanya, let him speak!"

The girl with long auburn hair came up to where I had been made to kneel in order to rip off the tape that held the panties in my mouth. I cried out as the sodden material fell from my mouth for the pain of the tape being removed caught me by surprise.

"Poor little boy upset by the tape coming off?" said the Captain nastily. "That's nothing compared to what we are going to do with you now though."

She went on to explain to me that hers was a much valued

45

infantry unit because her soldiers always got results for the dreaded NKVD, the Soviet secret police. Her troops never failed to extract all the information that the authorities required one way or another so they were allowed to play with the enemy soldiers that they captured for as long as they wished.

The man that I had seen before was a German commando who had been captured attempting to destroy Russian supply boats crossing the Volga. He had been persuaded to reveal the whereabouts of his fellow commandos after being strung up naked for two days and flogged to within an inch of his life by the captain.

Her troops were going to go out and check out the validity of his story but if they could not find his men he would be brought back for more special treatment at the hands of the captain.

"We have Germans, Italians and even Rumanians here," continued the captain boastfully. "In fact one of the men you doubtless saw in those hanging cages is from Sicily with his colleague from Rome. They refused to tell me where the weaknesses are in the Axis line north of Stalingrad."

"But they are protected..."

"They lost their protection when they fell into my hands," snapped the captain. "Now they talk or their balls will fry!"

She then proceeded to ask me how many Me. 110s there were at my airbase near the Don River but I flatly refused to answer. She seemed quite pleased at my reluctance for it meant that she could turn to her methods of persuasion to make me talk.

"Natasha, lower that rope so that we can stretch this arrogant pup's arms up his back to get the ball rolling here!" ordered the captain.

"Yes, Miss," answered the girl with the dark bob who had obviously been granted her wish to take part in my torture.

46

She brought a hook on the end of a long rope down behind my back before attaching it to the cords that still bound my wrists tightly together. Once it was secured she started to draw the other end of the rope down through a pulley system that immediately caused my arms to jerk painfully up behind me.

As Natasha pulled harder I found my wrists being raised to the level of my shoulders, which pushed my defenceless buttocks out for the attention of the eager crowd. She only stopped when my hands were dragged up behind me causing me to stand on tiptoe to avoid actually hanging by my aching wrists.

"Now do you feel like talking or do we have to add to your torment to loosen your tongue?" asked the captain, no doubt hoping that I would hold out for even more rough treatment.

"I will never tell you want you want to know," I said without much conviction in my voice.

"Oh but you will," replied the captain. "They all do in the end!"

With that she ordered her faithful sidekick Natasha to bring in the special device that she was so pleased to inform me had been designed to torture her prisoners. What Natasha wheeled into the room turned out to be an industrial sized fan on casters with four large metal blades. To each blade was attached a long thin strip of leather which made me shiver as I realised what the captain intended to do with it.

"What do you think of my lovely new toy?" asked the captain slyly.

"You'll never make me talk!" I cried, fearing now that this contraption would make me a liar.

"By the time this machine has finished with your cute bottom, you'll want to tell us everything including Hitler's current whereabouts," boasted the captain.

She explained that the fan would be faced upwards before being switched on, to its lowest setting at first. They had rigged the machine so that the direction of the blades would be reversed every minute, whether the operator was there or not.

In the distance I heard an electricity generator fire up, which would provide the power to drive the contraption behind me. Ridiculously I found myself thinking what an extravagant waste of fuel just to torture me but the captain standing by my side with her gloved finger on the switch soon sobered my thought process.

"I will turn this on and then my comrades and I will leave you to suffer on your own for a while," she said. "You will scream for mercy after a few minutes but I assure you that no one will come for at least half an hour - we have things to do to your friend first."

"But you can't leave me here like this..." I pleaded pathetically.

"Oh, but we can - contact!" she cried before throwing the switch on the dreaded mechanism.

All the girls laughed at my predicament as the captain led her platoon from the room as the machine whirred into life slowly but surely behind me. They laughed even more loudly because I yelped as the leather belts began to strike my left buttock with loud thwacks, which my perverse logic told me indicated that the fan was going clockwise on its first revolutions.

Why my mind kept filling with practical nonsense when I was in tricky situations I could not tell, but perhaps it was a coping device of some sort. As the stinging pain spread across my cheeks I realised that I was going to have to come up with some way of dealing with the flogging machine or else I knew I would go crazy after thirty minutes.

I tried to think of some of the whores that I had encountered during the various campaigns I had been involved in since the Third Reich charged into Poland in '39'. There was one particular girl with very unusual talents that I had come across in Paris that managed to captivate my imagination even as the dreadful machine ground to a halt and changed direction.

She had had long blonde hair and had been able to do things with her tongue that I did not believe possible. For a few measly francs myself and a few of the other pilots from my squadron had celebrated the fall of France with Madam Du Champ and her girls in her seedy brothel in the outskirts of the city.

Annette, who was the tart that I had chosen, had performed very well, if slightly reluctantly for her German oppressor. I had even encouraged her with my riding crop as she worked on me with her mouth but now it seemed that the boot was very much on the other foot.

On this occasion I was the one writhing in agony under the whirling straps of the captain's diabolical invention. Even images of the lovely Annette could not shield me from the increasing anguish that I was suffering as the leather strips repeatedly impacted on my juddering buttocks.

First one way then the other the leather tanned my hide thoroughly until my eyes watered with the relentless barrage of abuse that my cheeks were having to absorb. I tried to dance away from the endless stings that rained down upon me but my roped arms, always painful, returned me to the spot where the mechanical pain inducer regained its grip on me.

As my posture forced me to stare between my legs I was astonished to note that my cock was growing at an alarming rate. Despite the fact that I was experiencing excruciating pain across both cheeks of my bottom I had a huge erection which I simply could not explain.

I was also experiencing the great frustration of not being able to do anything about it because of my bonds. It seemed that my efforts to take my mind off my troubles had been too effective for now I had an uncontrollable hard-on. At that moment the captain and some of her troops re-entered, although I noted that there were fewer than before because the others were out acting on the information forced out of the German commando.

"Well, well, look what we have here," she said mischievously. "It seems that our gallant airman has a liking for our new machine and that even though it has thrashed him for thirty minutes solid, he actually enjoyed it!"

I took it as a good sign that the girls in the room laughed at their fearless leader's remarks although I could tell that she wasn't happy that I clearly hadn't been softened up by her methods so far. I saw a look in her eyes that told me she was already dreaming up another scheme to try and break me.

"Turn off the machine Tanya, and then show him what he'll be missing for a long time," she demanded of her favourite skivvy. "And re-gag him whilst you're at it!"

"Yes, Miss," replied Tanya, scampering over to where I was still semi-suspended next to the still whirring machine.

She flicked the switch to end the flogging for which I was very grateful but she did nothing to relieve the wrenching ache in my tortured shoulders. Instead she forced the sodden gag back into my mouth before sealing it again with more tape.

She then proceeded to fall to her knees in front of me in order to take my swollen member in her small but firm hands. I gasped as she looked up at me with her soft brown eyes before licking the end of my cock with her long well- practised tongue. Still keeping her eyes fixed firmly on mine she proceeded to slip my rock hard penis between her lips and into the soft wet interior of her mouth.

I moaned with pleasure despite my painful position for this girl had obviously given blow jobs to men before. She twirled her tongue round the stiff shaft of my tool, all the while sucking gently on the whole thing.

50

Despite the fact that I was doubled in two and it hurt to do so I began to thrust my hips forward so my cock was pushed down towards her throat. Tanya seemed to take this well even though the tip of my member actually touched the back of her throat. She simply ran her fingers up my trembling thighs and carried on serving me in the most tantalising way imaginable, a way that even Annette would have been proud of.

Realising that I was close to coming I began to shove my cock in and out of her mouth as I groaned loudly. I felt great because I knew it was going to become to be a fantastic, unexpected pleasure in amongst all this misery but Tanya stopped what she was doing to me seconds before I was going to shoot my load into her mouth.

She pulled back at the last moment leaving my rampant penis with her saliva dripping from it but no sign of my semen. I tried to implore her with my eyes to finish the job that she had so ably started but she just turned away from me so that she could return to her captain's side.

"So the whipping only turned you on," said the captain thoughtfully. "But little Tanya here drove you to thinking about giving away military secrets for a chance to come in her mouth!"

She was right of course, even though I did not want to admit it, but I would have told the exact number of aircraft that we had next to the Don River if only I had been allowed to have an orgasm. With a little fortitude I could have survived the whipping machine a lot longer but if Tanya came forward again to torment me I knew I would break instantly.

The captain realised this as well but for some reason she didn't follow through her advantage but instead ordered the reluctant Natasha to lower my arms. Perhaps she wanted to break me later but she ordered Natasha to take me back to the cell so that she could put me in my tiny box again to think about my position.

51

I looked at Tanya as I left and I was surprised to see a hint of regret in her face. Perhaps she didn't really enjoy being used to torture the captain's victims quite as much as Natasha clearly did. Maybe she actually wanted to swallow my come rather than tormenting me by taking my cock out of her eager mouth.

My fantasies about Tanya's willingness to suck my cock to orgasm were rudely interrupted as Natasha forced me into my box once more. Once I was squashed down into my minuscule wooden prison to the extent that my heels rubbed against my inflamed welt-covered bottom.

With a click of the padlock I was secured again with only the air holes through which to observe what was happening to my fellow prisoners. When I squinted through the tiny opening I could only see one man hanging by his wrists as naked as the day he was born.

He was facing me so I could see that his genitalia had been bound tightly by thin wire so that his cock hung limp before him. His head was bowed in humiliation but I recognised the man from the colour of his hair as well as the tattoo on his forearm above his head - it was Karl.

As I watched helplessly Natasha walked over to him in order to start stroking his cock with the tip of the riding crop that the captain had obviously lent her. Without any warning she suddenly brought the crop down with a mighty whoosh across his flaccid member.

Poor Karl screamed into his gag with all his might as a vivid scarlet line began to appear diagonally across his quivering cock. He tried in vain to turn away from his assailant but Natasha simply raised the crop again in order to deliver yet another devastating blow to Karl's penis.

I was so incensed about my comrade's treatment that I started to knock against the side of my box with my shoulders to attract the bitch's attention. In response to my frenzied efforts to

52

make her stop she just turned to where my box stood in order to give me a withering look of pure malice.

As if to prove that she was the one in total control of the situation she struck Karl's cock one more time before cutting him down with her bayonet. He fell in a crumpled heap at her feet, desperately grasping his crotch to try and stem the flow of pain from his throbbing member.

Natasha threw the customary rope around his neck so that she could drag him to his feet. With another disdainful look in my direction she pulled her new toy from the cell area, no doubt towards more ill-treatment at the hands of the captain.

I shouted uselessly into my gag at the retreating couple for I was so frustrated at being left helplessly in my box once more. My cock was still hard but the fact that my hands were still bound behind my back ensured that I could do nothing about it.

I could hear the groans of other tormented men in the room with me but I had not seen the two Italians in their candle lit cages as Natasha had brought me back in. Perhaps their information had proved correct or maybe the girls had decided to torture them in a different way whilst their revelations were acted upon.

In an effort to see more of the room I shuffled my head round in the tight confines of my damn box. Through another air hole I could just make out the two men lying next to each other on the ground at the far end of the chamber. They were in obvious agony but at first I could not see why. Then it suddenly came clear to me what their latest travail was as I spotted a series of ropes leading up to pulleys hanging from the ceiling. The men had been tied spread eagled to eye bolts in the floor with thin ropes but the problem they faced stemmed from the way the girls had dealt with their genitalia.

The wire was still tightly wrapped around their balls and

53

the base of their cocks but thin ropes had now been secured to them. These ropes practically bisected the poor men's testicles as they led up to the pulleys high above the prone victims.

At the other end of the ropes were attached sturdy metal trays which already contained several metal weights and these pulled down with constant pressure on the pulleys overhead. This in turn forced the men's balls upward with irresistibly agonising force and this was obviously the reason for the groaning coming from behind the men's panty gags.

As I studied the Italians' latest predicament I heard more groaning from the other side of my box so I turned round to peer through another of the air holes. In the unnerving glow of a single candle I saw the commando that I had witnessed being tortured before.

This time he was suspended upside down with his legs spread grotesquely wide by long ropes which were secured over a bar high above him. His hands were bound behind him and his gag was still firmly in place, although his muffeld groans could be heard.

With a sudden start I realised just where the candle had been placed and why the poor man was groaning so much. The girls had bound him in such a way that they had been able to insert the large candle into his rectum.

As the candle burnt ever downwards a steady trickle of wax was deposited painfully on the sensitive skin around his anus. Each droplet brought him more agony which he communicated to the rest of us as loudly as he could through his gag.

Suddenly two girls burst into the chamber with their brown uniforms all spattered with mud. They were bathed in sweat as they fought for breath but they did not let this put them off their purpose for being there.

"There was nobody there, you lying bastard," cried a particularly attractive blonde corporal. "Now we're going to make you pay for making us risk our lives for nothing!"

1 She slapped the man's backside with as much force as she could muster which sent a shower of melted wax over his up-turned legs. He moaned loudly as he swung backwards and forwards with the power of the blow she had dealt him.

With a supreme effort she rammed the candle further into his bottom causing him to scream even louder with the increased pain. He could not prevent her from defiling him in this way nor could he expel the candle from his anus.

"Now you can contemplate your lies as we decide how to punish you next," said the corporal menacingly as the scalding wax continued to build up upon his flesh after a much shortened journey.

With that she walked past my box to where the two Italians lay scared stiff at what the girls might do to them next.

"As for you, you pizza-guzzling dogs," she spat at the prostrate men. "You are going to tell us where the weak points are in the Italian line and this is why."

She ordered the other girl with her, a dark haired pretty creature, to fetch some more weights as the Italians cringed with fear below her. Once the girl came back the blonde corporal proceeded to place the small but heavy weights on the trays, which added to the pressure on the balls of her victims.

Each new weight added to the overall load on the Italians' scrotums elicited a fresh new groan that echoed around the draughty chamber. But the corporal continued with her task, undeterred by the fact that the Italians' scrotal sacs were already stretched above their heaving pelvises.

They feebly tried to lift themselves up in their bondage to alleviate the increasing pressure but were invariably forced down onto their backs again when they couldn't take the strain on their muscles any longer.

They didn't seem to realise that this activity made no difference to their suffering as the pulleys ensured that the weights applied the same pressure on their genitals whatever they did. Eventually they gave up the fight for they lay there moaning uselessly as the corporal continued to place the weights on the trays.

It was not until the Italians' balls had turned a deepest red and were stretched several inches away from their bodies that the corporal stopped adding weights. Perhaps she did not want their genitalia to be ripped off completely but it already looked as though they were heading that way.

I shivered in my box because I wondered what the hell they could dream up next for the two men, that could possibly be worse than they were already suffering. If this was the precursor to the actual chastisement then I dreaded to think what would be done to them eventually.

My sympathies for my two allies were cut short however when the girl looked over to my box with her piercing green eyes that were filled with hate.

"Bring that!" she ordered before flouncing out of the room without another word.

I was relieved that the other girl was not in as foul a mood as the corporal but I still did not wish to try my luck with the dark haired beauty. Instead I humbly climbed out of the box to place myself in total submission at her feet. I wanted to keep my balls if at all possible so I didn't want to provoke any vicious punishments for myself.

With the usual rope around my neck I followed the girl back to the recreation room where the captain was assembled with most of her troops, including the unhappy corporal.

"So, as you saw, flyboy, that commando lied to us and he's now beginning his journey to hell and back," said the captain with a sinister voice as I was made to kneel in front of her.

56

"You, on the other hand, have not actually lied to us yet, but it is time that we heard you singing like a bird for us."

She nodded sagely to her Natasha who came forward to drag me to a chair in the middle of the room. Once there she tied my bound-together arms over the back of the chair whilst binding my ankles to the front legs. With my thighs cruelly spread I was completely helpless again and my cock hung before me like a sacrifice prepared for some mysterious altar.

"Now that we know just how much you enjoy having your cock sucked we thought about making your friend Karl suck it for you," said the captain mischievously. "But we could save that for later, if you were really naughty and continue to hold out on us."

I began to sweat as I thought of Karl kneeling between my legs slurping away at my cock. I knew that I would do anything to avoid that fate, but I didn't have to, for the captain had something else in mind for me.

"Instead we will let the lovely Tanya have another go at you, but this time we will let you watch your friend being flogged as she serves you!"

As Tanya made her way towards me I saw Natasha go off to bring the hapless Karl into the room with his hands tied behind his back. In addition to this I could see that his elbows had been drawn painfully together with wire so that he was forced to stick his chest out.

Natasha took him over to another chair which she made him bend over whilst she secured him in that most hazardous position. His legs had been spread by ropes as well but unlike me it seemed that he was not going to derive any pleasure from the planned proceedings.

I watched the girls lining up, resplendent in their uniforms and their patent leather boots as little Tanya took my cock in her hands once more. I felt every sympathy for Karl when I saw the long switches made from thin strips of wood that they were all seemingly going to use on him but I suspected that I would enjoy every second of the coming travail.

How wrong I was for the captain had no intention of giving me any pleasure this time, any more than the first time Tanya had my cock in her mouth. This was simply going to be a test as to which of us would break first for it appeared that Karl could not stand being beaten as much as I hated being denied an orgasm.

Tanya produced a thin piece of wire which she used to wrap around the base of my balls a few times. This would help her to ensure that I did not come so that my torture could be prolonged for as long as possible. As she bound my balls she looked into my eyes with that same twinge of regret that I had seen before as if to show that she did not really want to do this to me again.

"Take off your top, little Tanya, just so the good captain can see your assets as you tease his manhood with your tongue!" ordered the captain.

Tanya looked round at her captain briefly but quickly divested herself of her brown tunic when she realised just how serious the command had been.

My vulnerable cock practically jumped for joy as her pert breasts spilled out from under the top half of her uniform. Her pink nipples were already hardening with the exposure to the cool air in the room but also, I fancied, from the prospect of what she was about to do to me.

She tried to cover herself but a loud tut from her captain made her turn her attentions back to her work. Again she took my cock, which was by this time already rampant, in her hands. Once more she carefully placed my manhood in her mouth keeping her submissive doe like eyes on mine as she did so.

The warm wet interior of her mouth combined with her

endlessly darting tongue made me want to come straight away but the skilfully placed wire prevented me ejecting my seed. Instead all I felt was the uncomfortable build-up of pressure in my balls that I was unable to relieve.

Tanya began to suck my swollen tool for all she was worth but I was still denied an orgasm by the unrelenting wire around my balls. I tried to thrust upwards from my chair but this didn't take me any closer to the thing I most craved.

In the meantime the other girls had started their assault on Karl's buttocks with their thin whippy switches. The room echoed to the loud thwacking sounds from the girls' chastising rods, interspersed with loud groans from Karl as he vented his pain into his panty gag.

I couldn't help but watch because the bright red lines began to multiply across his ruby cheeks as each girl took her turn to extract her own brand of revenge upon their helpless prey. Every stroke made the poor fellow jerk forward in fresh agony. Unfortunately for me the sight of all those strapping young maidens in their tight uniforms thrashing away at Karl's naked bottom only served to excite me even further with more unrequited lust. But even though Tanya was using her mouth as skilfully as she knew how, no amount of oral stimulation was going to enable me to come.

The captain certainly knew what she was doing with the pair of us for she simply sat there and laughed at our feeble attempts to cope with her latest torturous endeavours. I noticed that she was even taking the time to casually finger herself through the canvas of her pants.

She was obviously enjoying the spectacle unfolding before her for I could see her eyes glazing over as she concentrated on pleasuring herself. Her fingers moved furiously between her legs as she tried to stimulate her clitoris but she quickly realised that the thick material was too prohibitive.

Not wanting to spoil her own fun the captain unfastened her trousers so that she could slip her fingers down inside. Once she had located her hard bud I saw her close her eyes with a look of pure pleasure on her face as she replaced the scene before her with her own innermost thoughts.

This only heightened my own frustration as I desperately tried to shoot my load into the mouth of the pretty girl kneeling at my feet. I even tried in vain to raise myself up from my chair so I could thrust my cock deeper down her throat but the treacherous wire thwarted all my efforts to gain satisfaction.

To distract me I looked over to where Karl was receiving the worst thrashing of his life. He was screaming almost continuously into his panty gag but the women continued with their onslaught despite his muffled cries.

They wanted to break him so that he would give up his information plus they sought revenge for all the bombing that the Luftwaffe had been doing over mother Russia. As I looked at his tortured and much-striped body I realised that he was not far from giving up what few secrets we had to his tormentors.

At this point I heard a loud cry from the captain's direction as her efforts between her legs caused her to come unashamedly. She had a look of pure bliss on her face as the rush of pleasure blasted through her taut body.

"Stop what you are doing, immediately," she ordered, once she had recovered from her shattering orgasm. "I want to check if either of them are ready to talk, so take out their gags."

I gasped once more as little Tanya pulled the tape from my face, although I noticed that she did try to do it as carefully as she could. The panties slid from my mouth to the floor but all I was interested in was taking welcome deep breaths for a change.

"So, you pieces of filth, are you ready to talk or do we carry on like this?" she asked simply.

I shook my head in response for although my cock was fit for bursting and I was frustrated almost beyond all endurance I was not quite ready to betray my country. I could see Tanya practically pleading with me with her soft brown eyes but I did not relent for I knew that I would not be able to live with myself if I did.

Karl on the other hand had clearly had enough for he began to beg for mercy whilst offering to tell the captain anything she wished to know. I snarled at him that he was a traitor but Natasha stormed over to me in order to slap my face with the back of her hand.

"Silence, scum," she yelled, slapping the other side of my face for good measure.

"Gag that one again for we do not want him interfering with this," snapped the captain with her eyes fixed on the one prisoner that she had broken.

Natasha stuffed the wet panties back into my mouth, securing them once more with a length of surgical tape.

"Now, flyboy, tell us what you know," said the captain sweetly, not wanting to put him off just yet.

Karl proceeded to tell the captain about all the aircraft we had by the Don River as well as details of ammunition and fuel supplies. I tried to break free of my bonds to stop him but the ropes held me secure.

"Tanya, give him something else to think about whilst his comrade spills the beans," ordered the captain.

Tanya understood the order for she took my swollen member into her soft wet mouth once more. Again her tongue lashed my cock but at least I could still tell from her eyes that she was abusing me under duress.

I tried to take my mind off the return of the build-up of pressure in my balls by thinking of Karl's treachery but it did not work. All I could think of was the sweet little creature between my legs sucking my cock and it made me want to come even more.

The poor girl was driving me out of my mind with frustration but I consoled myself with the knowledge that she had no choice but to tease me so. She did not mean to make me suffer this way and I was convinced that she would gladly swallow every drop of my come if she were allowed to.

Eventually Karl seemed to run out of things to say so the captain called a halt to the whole proceedings and had him re-gagged. She told her troops to take us back to the cells where we would be left for the night but that along with the lying commando I was to be given nothing when the rest of the 'animals' were fed.

We were thrown still bound into individual cells that occu-pied the far wall after being returned to the room. As the girls had not bothered to remove the gags we could not talk with one another so I contented myself by looking round the torture chamber again.

I noticed that the Italians were no longer bound on the floor having their balls wrenched off so I assumed that they were next door. The commando was still suspended upside down in the far corner but the candle was only a couple of inches above his quivering cheeks.

Nobody appeared to care about his plight so it looked as though the flame would only be extinguished once it had burnt its way into his anus. I could hear the poor fellow sobbing as he realised that his attempts to protect his comrades had earned him unenviable torment.

I winced as more wax dropped onto his flesh but I was distracted by the arrival of a couple of girls with what passed for the evening meal. I was beginning to feel very hungry for I hadn't eaten since we left our base. The food may not have looked appealing but I would have scoffed the lot given the chance.

As I looked on with ravenous eyes as the first cell door was opened to allow one of the Italians to crawl out. His hands were bound behind him so it was a real struggle for him to lean forward in order to slurp up the grey liquid slopped into the bowl placed on the floor in front of him.

The girls prodded him with the butts of their guns as he ate for they were obviously keen to get this odious task over with. Once his bowl was empty they repeated the process with the other Italian, then a Rumanian corporal, wearing only his distinctive cavalry boots and finally with Karl.

I was disgusted at the way he grovelled at the girls' feet like a grateful dog and lapped up his meagre meal. At one point some of the gruel fell from his mouth onto one of the girls' boots and he licked off the slime even without being ordered to.

The girls laughed at his prostrate naked form and simply kicked him back into his cell when he had licked his bowl clean. Just as with the other prisoners the guards replaced Karl's gag before locking him away behind the bars of his small cell.

"No food for this one," said the more attractive of the two guards. "And the same goes for that lying bastard over there!"

"What shall we do about the candle?" asked the fair haired soldier looking at the suffering commando.

"Nothing - it will teach him not to lie to the sisters of the Red Army," said the senior guard, turning on her heels to leave us in the darkness of the improvised torture chamber.

I tried to sleep on the cold concrete floor of the cell, however I found myself transfixed by the flickering candle between the legs of the groaning commando. I could still make out his tortured frame in the dim light but I was relieved to note that as the flame finally reached the stretched skin of his anus it was snuffed out.

63

As the room descended into total blackness the poor commando let out one mighty scream into his gag for the flame must have scorched his flesh badly before being extinguished. His muffled cries echoed through the dark room unsettling all the doomed occupants of that fearful hellhole.

In fact his yells haunted my dreams when I finally fell into a fitful slumber only to be rudely awoken in the very early hours of the next morning when different guards burst into the chamber.

They had come for me, for it appeared that I was the only one of their captives who had not spoken as yet. The two girls dragged me along a corridor to a small room that I had not seen before where they dumped me on the floor to await whatever the captain had in store for me.

As I lay on the floor waiting, my wrists hurt from being continuously bound for over twenty four hours, which added to the discomfort of how hungry I was feeling. My stomach churned but I knew that it was not only my appetite for I actually began to shiver with fear at the prospect of what was going to happen next.

I jumped as the captain rushed into the room slamming the door behind her with a deafening bang. The fact that she was on her own did nothing to calm my fears for it was clear that she had something painful in mind for me.

"I think that it is high time you started talking, don't you?" she asked menacingly.

I shook my head as usual, hoping that my defiance would last out this latest period of questioning by my captor.

"You see, my girls have prepared something especially for you next door that combines pain with pleasure, which I know you're going to hate, so why not speak before I let them loose on you?" she continued in a disturbing pleasant manner.

Again I shook my head vigorously, which quickly brought

to an end her all too brief attempt to persuade me into submission.

She called for some of her girls to assist her and I was soon being dragged along the corridor to yet another room that I had not seen before.

It was the same size as the last one but there were several guards waiting for me inside as well as a very strange device made of cold grey metal. My heart was racing as they took me over to the contraption which consisted of a narrow pole sticking up three feet vertically attached a short crossbeam a few inches from the floor.

At the ends of the horizontal pole were short leather straps with buckles but what sent shivers down my spine was the fact that at the end of the vertical pole was a strange bullet shaped object. I had a funny feeling that I knew where it was meant for and this was confirmed as the girls manhandled me.

I was lifted up by the girls until my bottom was above the spike upon which I could see one of the girls smearing what looked like lubricant. I tried to struggle but there were too many of them, including an extremely determined Natasha who seemed keen to guide me onto my dreadful perch.

As the well-oiled invader reached the entrance to my anus I cried out for the girls simply pulled on my legs and forced it all the way into my rectum. The blast of pain was excruciating but the girls hadn't finished their task for they next turned to the straps that would keep me in agony.

My legs were yanked brutally apart so that they could fasten my ankles with short leather belts at each end of the crossbar. This had the effect of taking my feet off the floor so that most of my weight pressed down onto the huge dildo deep inside me.

I could not believe that such anguish was possible as my internal muscles fought to prevent me from being torn in two.

My muffled screams filled the room but the girls only laughed at the torment they had contrived for me as most of them trooped out of the room .

Eventually only Natasha remained who looked at me with hatred in her eyes as I struggled to cope with the distress that the device was causing me.

"No Tanya to suck your cock this time, big boy," she said with pure venom in her voice. "This thing will sort you out - talk or we will leave it to work its way slowly deeper up inside you."

Even though I was suffering badly I still managed to shake my head again so she stalked off to find more malleable prey to play with.

Meanwhile I was left to endure the worst pain I had ever experienced in my life as the dildo continued its inexorable journey upward inside me. I tried in vain to reach for the floor but there was no relief to be gained in that direction.

Just as I gave up all hope of being saved from my predicament after hours of torture young Tanya entered the room with a slightly nervous look on her face and carrying two small boxes. She immediately knelt before me to place the boxes under my feet so that I could stand again, which brought instant relief to my tortured rectum. She then looked up at me with her large brown eyes before moving to undo the straps that bound my ankles.

I shook my head and looked down at my cock which was becoming erect at the sight of the lovely Tanya at my feet once more. I tried to indicate that she should carry on our unfinished business, a fact that she seemed to appreciate for she took my cock in her hands for a third time. She lovingly caressed my stiffening tool before slipping it between her parted lips and into her welcoming mouth. I tugged on my bonds in delight as she started to suck with all the skills that the captain had doubtless made poor Tanya learn in her service.

With every swirl of Tanya's wicked tongue I groaned my pleasure into my ever-present panty gag but it was the relentless sucking that took me to the very edge of the abyss.

I even tried to hold out so as I could prolong my own pleasure but Tanya grabbed my balls with one hand whilst stroking my aching buttocks with the other. As she gently squeezed my unfettered balls I felt the inevitable build-up of pressure to the extent that I knew I could no longer contain myself.

As I came I felt the rush of excitement flood through me and I joyfully spurted my semen against the back of Tanya's throat. Tanya swallowed every drop of what I had to offer her before she began to unfasten the straps that dug into my ankles whilst still licking her lips. She seemed delighted to have had the chance to taste my seed for she had a broad smile on her lovely face.

I could not understand why this girl who was supposed to be my mortal enemy would risk the end of solidarity with her comrades by making me come. She would be in a lot of trouble with her fellow soldiers if they ever discovered what she had done for me.

Gently she helped me to manoeuvre myself off my painful perch then pulled the panty gag from my mouth, which she threw into the corner in disgust.

"Thank you, Tanya," I whispered once I had recovered my voice after being gagged for so long.

"It is not a problem," she replied in her thick Russian accent, "but now we must get out of here!"

"Where are we going?" I asked, surprised at another display of her solidarity with her enemy.

"I am getting you out of here so you can go home," she said simply.

"But what about you?" I asked, knowing full well that the

captain would make her pay for her treachery.

Tanya explained that her friend was covering for her and that the captain would never know what had happened here. She had to lead me out with my hands still bound, just in case anyone saw us, but she was confident that we could get out unseen.

After she had opened the door I followed her, still naked and with my head still full of questions but it was clear that Tanya was not going to explain her actions to me as she led me away. I walked on in silence following my saviour as closely as I could.

Once we had reached the outside of the building Tanya took me to a small shed in which she had placed some clothes earlier in the day. It was already dark as we traversed the shattered landscape and I was acutely embarrassed to be out in the cold evening air without any clothes on.

Inside the shed Tanya moved as if to undo my bonds but I shook my head for I wanted to repay her somehow for her bravery.

"Look, I want to pay you back for what you have done for me, but this is all I have," I said quietly, looking down at my cock which was already rock hard again with all the excitement.

Tanya simply smiled at me before quickly removing her uniform revealing her small firm breasts as well as her neatly trimmed bush. I was enchanted by the way her nipples immediately hardened in the cold shed however her deep brown eyes still captivated me most.

She did not bother to untie me but simply pushed me backwards on to a pile of sacks whilst kissing me fiercely on my mouth. Tanya obviously wanted to control me by herself prior to setting me free so I made no attempt to struggle.

I lay back as she straddled my body before sliding herself

down onto my rampant cock. I could feel that the lips of her sex were already moist with her dew as she thrust my shaft deep into her sodden pussy. She groaned loudly as she began to bounce up and down wantonly on my manhood and her gorgeous eyes misted over in her passion. Her breasts bounced in a most charming way as she urged herself on to the orgasm that she was almost as desperate to attain as I had been.

Moments before we were both nearing our climaxes Tanya reached forward in order to pinch my nipples as hard as she could. The pain was exquisite but it was exactly what I required to send me over the edge into my second overwhelming orgasm of the evening. This time I shot my semen deep within her quivering sex as she shared the experience that I was going through. Waves of delight engulfed us both as our senses were pushed beyond the realms of mere ecstasy. Just for that brief moment in the midst of the bitterness of the Eastern Front campaign Tanya and I were as one. Even though I was bound I was happy to be totally under the spell of this beguiling girl who felt compelled to release me but who, for that instant was my all consuming mistress.

Eventually Tanya broke the spell as she pulled herself from me leaving a sticky trail from her pussy behind her. She smiled as she put her drab uniform back on, preferring silence as an end to our forbidden union. Once she was dressed she untied me so that I could put on the clothes that she had stashed in the corner of the shed. I did not say a word as I donned the clothes for I did not want to spoil the moment.

When we had finished dressing Tanya led me over the wasteland again towards the river where she had hidden a small boat earlier in the day.

"Alright Fritz, this is your way out," she said, resigned to the fact that I had to go.

"But Tanya, can't we...?" I began somewhat pathetically.

"No, you must go," urged Tanya. "If you go now I will get away with what I have done but if you delay..."

I kissed her on her cheek before jumping into the boat. As I rowed away from her I watched her face, which was impassive but which I knew was hiding the full gamut of emotions with which I was coping. She was out of sight long before I reached the other shore but her face was still in my mind as I scrambled ashore.

I would have thought about her a lot more as I wandered into the battered city but I soon discovered that the Russians had broken through the Italian and Rumanian lines and that Paulus' Sixth Army was surrounded. Perhaps the Italians in the loving care of the captain had cracked after all with their vital information.

My heart skipped a beat as I realised that I might fall into Russian hands again and that I might just end up at the mercy of little Tanya once more.

"Of course Reginald used to let me flog the maids and some of the soldiers' wives when we were in India, you know," said Lady Julia Hamilton-Smythe to her friend and confidante, Lucinda Spencer.

"Really, I didn't think that sort of thing was allowed," replied Lucinda, aghast at what she had heard.

1"Well, when your husband is Colonel in charge of the supply column heading towards Wellesley you can do pretty much what you want," said Julia complacently.

"Yes, I can see that flogging the maids might be acceptable, but the wives of the redcoats?" asked Lucinda, still sceptical about her colleague's outrageous claims.

"If you doubt my word then you can ask Reginald himself , when he gets back from his latest mission!" retorted Julia, slightly offended that her friend would question her word.

"No, darling, I believe you," said Lucinda hastily. "It's just that it all sounds a little far fetched, that's all."

"Well it is true and very enjoyable it all was too," said Julia huffily.

"Tell me about it then dear, for it all sounds terribly exciting," begged Lucinda who was already jealous that her friend had been allowed to whip other people.

"There were so many, I just wouldn't know where to begin," responded Julia mischievously.

She knew full well that her companion was extremely keen on hearing her tales from India, especially those that involved the punishment of the lower ranks.

The two ladies had travelled extensively throughout Spain, following their husbands throughout the Peninsular War. They had shared their stories from their past many time as they were doing now over afternoon tea under the shade of a large parasol.

Lucinda had always found her older acquaintance's anecdotes much more interesting than her own for they were mainly made up of accounts of her time in the Indian sub-continent. She could talk for hours about her adventures but this latest topic seemed much more interesting as it involved the infliction of pain.

Ever since she had been a child Lucinda had been fascinated by the idea of punishment, both of herself as well as others. Her particular interest had been watching through the study door keyhole as her father flogged the serving girls.

She had of course been regularly beaten as well by her father, usually over his knee with his wicked looking dog whip. Every stroke had made her cry out for mercy but her father was strict, never letting her off once she had incurred his wrath.

Lucinda had often wondered what it would feel like to hold the whip with its short silver tipped handle in her grip. She had longed to be the one administering ferocious punishments perhaps to one of the younger butlers at home or even one of the stable lads.

Sadly she never had the chance to experience the delights of wielding the whip back at her father's estate in Berkshire. She had been married off to the handsome Captain Ian Spencer who had taken her off as a naÔve eighteen year old girl to the unfolding war in the Iberian Peninsular.

Now she feared that she would never have the chance wield a whip for as an officer's wife she found herself having to behave in such a terribly nice way. She was not even punished by her new husband because he was far too preoccupied with trying to impress his senior officers, including the Commander-in-Chief, Sir Arthur Wellesley.

In fact Lady Smythe was the one bright star in all the tedium of army life for she had her stories, stories which invariably involved some sexual intrigue including various accounts of public as well as private floggings. These were the ones that Lucinda was particularly interested in, but she had never heard any in which Lady Smythe had actually used the whip herself.

"Tell me about the first time you did it," pleaded Lucinda. "It must have been very exciting for you!"

"It was, although I was very apprehensive at first about the whole thing," replied Lady Smythe. "You see the Colonel and I had been in India for about three months when he received his orders. We made our way to meet the supply column that the Colonel was to command and it seemed pretty clear some firm discipline was needed to restore order."

Lady Smythe went on to explain to how the Colonel had selected several of the lazy drovers and guards at random for flogging on the infamous army triangle. A sound flogging had long been considered the best way to make soldiers behave like men, although some considered that it only taught men how to turn their backs.

Those selected had all been bound against the lances, which had been driven into the ground some six feet apart and lashed together at the apex with stout rope. Another lance, bound horizontally across the wooden shafts ensured stability when the flogging commenced.

The victims' wrists were secured to the tops of the lances whilst their ankles were cruelly spread before being tied to the base of each of the lances. The upper garments were removed, usually by being ripped to shreds so as there would be no protection for the victim from the full force of the whip.

A sergeant would then come forward in order to deliver the requisite number of strokes, anything up to two hundred for desertion, with the dreaded lash. This was composed of a short wooden handle attached to roughly a dozen viciously thin strands of leather all knotted at the end for the maximum painful effect.

Lady Smythe explained how she had stood in the heat of the late morning sun to watch the twenty men stripped and flogged in front of the assembled company of troops. Each had received only thirty lashes as an example to the rest before the column had resumed its journey northwards.

"This seemed to do the trick for the men fell into line properly after that, but by the time we reached the next village there was another matter to deal with," continued Lady Smythe, relishing her role as storyteller.

"A matter that necessitated another flogging?" asked Lucinda, wondering when they would come to the bit where Lady Smythe actually joined in the fun.

"Yes, my dear, they usually do require some sort of punishment, but this time I persuaded the Colonel to let me play a part," said Lady Smythe, her eyes alive with the excitement of her recollections.

"What did you do?" asked Lucinda, equally stimulated by Lady Smythe's memories.

Lady Smythe went on to tell Lucinda about four of the camp followers, wives of some of the common soldiers, who had gone ahead of the column to steal food from the villages. They wanted the food for their husbands before the quartermaster could buy it for all of the men.

The women had been caught in the act and brought before Colonel Smythe for summary judgement. He had pronounced them all guilty as charged with the sentence being twenty lashes for each on the triangle.

"At this point I innocently asked if I could deliver the strokes to add a woman's touch to the proceedings," proceeded Lady Smythe slyly. "The Colonel said that it was a splendid idea but that, as I wasn't as strong as the sergeant then the women would

74

have to receive forty each to ensure they were properly chastised."

"That's one hundred and sixty strokes between them," stammered Lucinda. "How on earth did you cope?"

"I rolled up my sleeves and took my time about the whole thing," replied Lady Smythe with a smile on her imperious face. "The only way to get through it was to get a steady rhythm going whilst stopping for breath every now and then."

Lady Smythe delighted in telling her younger listener how the hapless women were brought out to the centre of the village where the triangle had been erected. She was positively skittish when she explained how the first was bound to the frame with her wrists secured high above her pretty head. The young woman's feet had dangled just above the dusty earth as the guards tied her dainty ankles to the poles either side of her.

"Then, my dear, I approached the poor little thing and ripped her thin dress apart at the back," said Lady Smythe, breathless with excitement.

"Did she complain at being stripped like that in front of all those men?" enquired Lucinda, equally stimulated by the older woman's story.

"How could she, considering they had already gagged her with the thick wooden bit to prevent her biting her tongue?" replied Lady Smythe, winking at the wide eyed girl.

"Oh, I see," said Lucinda.

"That's right my dear, although she could still scream and she proved it as soon as I started to beat her," said Lady Smythe with a wide grin.

She described every detail of how her whip swished through the air to land on the helpless girl's back with a loud crack which seemed to resonate through the village. This echo was rapidly eclipsed by the sound of the girl yelling into her gag for mercy, a plea that Lady Smythe had resolutely ignored.

Instead she continued to scourge the wretched girl with all her might until she worked herself into a sweaty frenzy. As she thrashed away to her heart's content the sergeant meticulously counted the strokes up to the requisite forty.

"I was slipping into some sort of frenzy and the screams of that poor girl only made me more excited!" said Lady Smythe, panting as she recalled that first flogging. "The red marks appeared across her delicate skin with every stroke of the whip, making me even more determined to cover her entire back with them."

"How did it feel, to have all that power over a helpless victim?" Lucinda asked, desperate to discover what it was like to wield the whip in such a fashion.

"I don't know whether I should tell you this, my dear but it rather got my juices flowing," replied Lady Smythe, almost too embarrassed to mention her arousal in front of such company.

1"You mean it sexually aroused you?" asked Lucinda.

She found that her fascination with the subject of chastising others made her bold with her questions, perhaps beyond her station in society. She simply had to know what it was like to flog someone for real for she had only ever imagined it as part of her wildest fantasies.

"Yes my dear, I am ashamed to admit that it did!" replied Lady Smythe.

"Don't be ashamed, Lady Smythe, your secrets are safe with me," assured Lucinda. "Besides, I must confess that the very thought of beating someone makes me go all tingly inside."

"I know what you mean, my dear," replied Lady Smythe, relieved to have found someone like herself at last. "In fact as I whipped the wretched girl I was sure that I actually came close to an orgasm!"

"I sometimes do that to myself when Ian is away with his men," confessed Lucinda sheepishly. " I imagine that one of the prettier maids has spilled some red wine and I get to punish her."

"Sounds like a lot of fun," said Lady Smythe, even more attracted to this younger girl who seemed to think the same way she did.

"Then I rub my breasts and play with myself between my legs until I come," explained the red-faced Lucinda.

"Goodness, that's what I do as well," said Lady Smythe with a mischievous grin on her face. "But what do you think Captain Spencer would do to you if he ever found out?"

"No doubt he would give me the thrashing of my life, much worse than my father ever gave me!" replied Lucinda with a shiver.

"Oh, that sounds thrilling," said Lady Smythe. "Perhaps I should arrange it, with a little audience made up of the other officers' wives."

"No, I think not," said Lucinda hastily. "Anyway, you haven't finished telling me about the flogging you dealt out in India."

"Ah yes, India," breathed Lady Smythe dreamily. "It wasn't the only flogging I meted out, but it was the first and one of the most memorable."

Lucinda's ploy to divert her friend from her plans to have her publicly beaten had worked for Lady Smythe was transported back into the ethereal haze of her adventures in India.

She went on to explain how the first victim had been cut down, once the last stroke had been viciously delivered. The snivelling girl had been dragged away with her back a mass of angry red lines, much to the delight of the watching soldiers.

Lady Smythe told Lucinda how she had found herself fighting for breath as the next girl was brought struggling to the triangle by two burly redcoats. She remembered how she had struggled to control herself in front of all those uniformed men, but her excitement at the unfolding scenario almost made her forget herself as well as her rank.

She had watched intently as the second girl had been tightly bound in exactly the same way as the first one. Having witnessed the way Lady Smythe had flogged her partner-in-crime the young woman begged for mercy but this did not put the eager chastiser off the task ahead.

The girl's thin cotton shirt was ripped away by the guards, exposing her ample bosom to the delight of the crowd. Lady Smythe made a point of walking slowly round her victim to examine her breasts, which hung like heavy water melons, firm and very ripe.

Once she had inspected her prey Lady Smythe took up position behind the girl who was hopelessly straining against her bonds. With a quick look around at the attentive audience she raised her arm high in the hot dry air in order to begin the next bout of flogging.

A loud crack followed by a deafening scream signalled the arrival of the first stroke upon the girl's back. The white skin was quickly blemished with vivid red weals that made the girl look as though she had been mauled by a tiger.

She pulled even harder against her bonds but that only spurred her tormentor on for Lady Smythe explained to Lucinda how a blood lust had taken her over. She continued the scourging with more force than ever as the lash produced an intricate lattice work of scarlet whip marks.

"The Sergeant had to stop me for I went beyond the allotted number in my exuberance," continued Lady Smythe. "It was dreadfully embarrassing but I was enjoying myself so much that I forgot to listen to the count!"

"What happened next?"

"Well, they simply cut her down and dragged her away,"

replied Lady Smythe, not even troubled by the memory of the event.

"And the third one," enquired Lucinda. "Did they still let you deal with her?"

"Of course," said Lady Smythe. "The Colonel had said that I was to administer the punishment and so they had no choice but to let me continue."

"But weren't you hot and bothered by then in the heat of the day?"

"Yes I was, but I had to continue to save face," insisted Lady Smythe. "I knew that I had given the second girl at least half a dozen strokes too many but I had to impose my authority over the girls as well as over myself."

"So you went on to beat the third one," Lucinda encouraged.

"I certainly did and by the time her dress was torn apart at the back I was getting well into my stride," boasted Lady Smythe.

She told Lucinda that the third flogging had been a breeze for her and that the aching she had felt in her upper arm after the first two beatings had simply vanished. The whip had flowed backwards and forwards as if attached to a well-oiled machine as she had warmed to her role as camp chastiser.

There had been none of the awkwardness or fatigue that she had experienced before and it seemed that she had been born to mete out these severe punishments. The fourth girl had pleaded for mercy as the others had but Lady Smythe had coolly continued, relishing each stroke in turn.

Lady Smythe calmly explained how for the fourth time pale flesh was transformed into a mass of welts as the evil lash worked its way across the poor girl's back. She told the enthralled Lucinda how she had already become quite proficient with the whip, quickly able to make the tangle of leather straps

79

land exactly where she wanted them to.

"It was so easy for me to lay the lashes across marks I had previously made, which made the young woman cry out in agony even louder," said Lady Smythe gleefully.

"Oh my dear, how could you be so cruel?" asked Lucinda, surprised that her friend could be so bloodthirsty.

"You obviously haven't flogged anybody have you, my girl?" said Lady Smythe sagely. "Otherwise you wouldn't ask me such a question."

"What do you mean?" asked Lucinda.

"Well, if you ever find yourself in the position where you hold the power of pain or pleasure over another person then you will find out the answer to that question for yourself," replied Lady Smythe mysteriously.

"Pain or pleasure?" said Lucinda, totally confused after all the talk of young ladies in agony under the scourge.

"Well let me give you a little clue as to what I am getting at," said Lady Smythe with a twinkle in her eye. "Do you remember that I told you I had flogged a redcoat?"

"Yes, I thought that was what you were going to tell me about," responded Lucinda indignantly.

"A little patience, my dear," said Lady Smythe reproachfully. "All things come to those who wait!"

"Yes, I'm sorry," whispered Lucinda, instantly ashamed of herself. "Please, do go on, I do so love to hear your stories."

"I know you do, pretty one," said Lady Smythe, already feeling the hackles of her anger at the younger woman's impatience subsiding.

She moved to sit beside her friend Lucinda on the veranda of the Madrid town house, the one that her husband had commandeered for them when the British had captured the city, pleased that her companion looked no more than a young girl in the fading light of the setting sun.

Lady Smythe knew that she had so much to teach this girl with the long flowing blonde hair and innocent blue eyes. She may already have been married but her husband had not been able to spend much time with her so it was obviously the duty of her older and more experienced colleague to enlighten her.

Lucinda had listened so intently to all her tales from India, especially the ones about punishing the servants or the wives of the soldiers. The story of the flogging in the square of the Indian village had really excited the girl for she could see her nipples poking boldly through the printed cotton of her dress.

The time had come, perhaps she would initiate this girl into some of the activities that she was so obviously keen on. It was all very well to simply talk about the punishments that the Colonel had allowed her to administer in India, but the girl really ought to experience the thrill of a flogging for herself.

She decided then that she would tell Lucinda about scourging the redcoats in India before arranging with her dear Colonel for the young Lady to experience it in the flesh, one way or the other. Lady Smythe wondered whether the girl might actually acquire a taste for being beaten but she would have plenty of opportunities to discover that later.

The war in the Iberian Peninsular seemed set to go on for a long time yet and so long as Lucinda's gallant captain survived, she would have her young friend at her side and maybe even at her mercy. In the meantime her story of lashing a humble private would keep the girl's interest aflame.

"After I had finished with the four girls I was tremendously excited by the whole episode and ready to go off to my private tent," she continued. "But the Colonel had other plans for me."

"What did he want of you next?" asked Lucinda, breathless with anticipation.

"He decided that I should flog one of his soldiers who had been caught asleep on guard the previous night,"

"My goodness, so this is when you actually whipped a man," said the awe-struck Lucinda trying to take in the significance of the event.

"Well, he decided that being flogged by a woman would add to the punishment of the lazy brute by humiliating him in front of his colleagues," said Lady Smythe.

"Was he frightened when they brought him to the triangle?" asked Lucinda.

"No, not at all," said Lady Smythe. "You see, he had not witnessed the previous beatings and he thought that he would take his fifty lashes easily."

"Fifty lashes!" cried Lucinda. "That seems such a lot."

"Actually my husband was letting him off lightly," said Lady Smythe. "For sleeping on sentry duty the man should have had several times as many strokes but it was his first offence."

"Golly, I see what you mean," said Lucinda, again appalled at the cruelty that the army could display. She had been so stimulated by all of Lady Smythe's tales that she could hardly control herself now as she sat so close to the imposing story-teller. She felt a strange yearning in her stomach that she had not encountered since she had first met her dashing husband two years previously.

Lucinda had never really come to terms with her fascination with punishment, both of others as well as herself. She longed to hold the whip and yet part of her wanted to lift up the hem of her dress so that she could offer herself to Lady Smythe for instant chastisement for being such a naughty little girl. Her mind whirled as she considered all the possibilities of being tormentor or tormented and she simply couldn't make up her mind. It was clear that Lady Smythe enjoyed having the whip hand but Lucinda was not so sure of her position in the relationship of power over subservience.

"The lad was still sure of himself as they tied him to the

triangle, but he soon changed his mind when I started to flog him," said Lady Smythe imperiously.

"I bet he did," declared Lucinda, her mind snapping back from confusion to clarity as she listened to Lady Smythe's story.

"Once his shirt had been stripped from his back I began, like a woman possessed, to flog him," continued Lady Smythe. "He screamed into his gag like a little baby but I carried on with the beating trying to make each stroke harder than the last."

"What did it feel like to be able to do that to a man, especially in front of all those people?" enquired Lucinda.

"It was simply marvellous, my dear, you wouldn't believe what it does for the constitution!" laughed Lady Smythe as she recalled how just how aroused she had become during the course of the flogging.

"I bet he wasn't so cocky after you'd finished with him, was he?"

"He certainly wasn't, the slovenly lout," replied Lady Smythe. "In fact I soon had him pleading for mercy, which made me feel even more invigorated!"

"And you managed to keep going for the full fifty lashes?" enquired Lucinda even though she suspected that she already knew the answer.

"Of course I did, my dear," replied Lady Smythe with a huge grin on her face. "In fact I finished the whole thing off with a flourish!"

"Why, what on earth did you do to him?"

"Well, when the count had reached forty nine I performed a little pirouette," confided Lady Smythe. "Then, with a mighty blow I brought the whip down between the man's shoulder blades across all the other bright red stripes that I had already put there!"

"Oh! I bet that upset him," said Lucinda, cringing as she

83

thought of the agony that the stroke must have inflicted on the already suffering soldier."

"You can say that again," Lady Smythe chuckled merrily. "If he hadn't been tied so tightly to the triangle he would have shot several yards into the air!"

Lucinda found herself laughing at this poor man's predicament even though he must have been cast adrift on a sea of pain, especially with Lady Smythe's last blow. But what a wonderful experience it must have been to have had a man at her mercy with a whip in her hand.

She snuggled up to Lady Smythe who proceeded to put her arm around her shoulders in order to draw her even nearer. They were already close friends but somehow these stories were bringing them still closer together.

Whilst their husbands were away fighting the French in the mountains to the north of Madrid they had no one to turn to. They needed someone to fulfil the physical needs that kept them awake at night in the heat of the Spanish plains but alas, nightly, they went to their beds alone.

As they held each other tight they considered the stories that Lady Smythe had been sharing. They both craved their men but also the opportunity to enter into the shady world where the whip held sway over the desires of those under its power.

"When were you last punished?" asked Lady Smythe out of the blue.

"Er...about three years ago," answered Lucinda hesitantly.

"By whom and what for?" persisted Lady Smythe.

"It was my father, he punished me for being cheeky to my mother, but why do you ask?" said Lucinda, increasingly wary of Lady Smythe's line of questioning.

"Oh, I am just curious, that's all, what did he do to you?"

"He had one of the male servants hold me over the back of

84

a chair whilst he beat me with his dog whip," said Lucinda, acutely embarrassed at letting Lady Smythe know what was supposed to be her secret.

"Did he whip you over your skirts or on your naked bottom?" Lady Smythe probed.

"He lifted my skirt over my head so that I could not see what was going on."

"So he hurt you, my dear," whispered Lady Smythe, stroking Lucinda's head as she caressed the answers out of her young friend. "How did it make you feel?"

"I was frightened as well a little ashamed to be punished in front of the man servant," continued Lucinda hesitantly. "Daddy hurt me with his horrible dog whip, leaving my buttocks covered with the kind of stripes you were talking about earlier."

"But there was something else, wasn't there?" insisted Lady Smythe, turning to look once again into the deep blue of the girl's eyes.

"Well, I am mortified to admit it but I was aroused by the whole episode," confessed Lucinda, her face as red as her buttocks had been when her father had finished chastising her.

"What do you mean by aroused?" Lady Smythe asked, determined to push this girl as far as she would go.

"You know, queasy yet happy inside."

"Do you mean that you were sexually aroused, so to speak?" suggested Lady Smythe wickedly. "To the extent that you were ready to go and play with yourself, as soon as they released you."

"How did you know?" Lucinda exclaimed, dismayed that her secret had been so easily extracted from her.

"I was once that confused little girl myself, over my father's knee and totally overwhelmed by the feelings the spanking was stirring up within me," said Lady Smythe, gently taking Lucinda's face in her hands.

"So you went off to, er, relieve yourself did you?" asked Lucinda shyly.

"Yes I did and I am not ashamed to say it for I led a very sheltered life and playing with myself was one of my few pleasures in life."

"Oh, wasn't it wonderful the way the pain made one so wet and hard?" said Lucinda dreamily. "I only had to touch myself between my legs and it sent shivers right through me."

"Would you like me to spank you now, my dear?" Lady Smythe offered.

"But I haven't done anything wrong," Lucinda protested.

"Oh but you have, you naughty little girl," asserted Lady Smythe. "You have just asked a lady about her most intimate habits and that is extremely mischievous!"

"But Lady Smythe, you were asking me..."

"No buts, young lady, get yourself over my knee, now!" the older woman ordered, her voice suddenly becoming domineering as well as a little menacing.

Lucinda dutifully stood up so that she could place herself humbly over Lady Smythe's knees. Once she was comfortable she placed the palms of her hands on the hard wooden floor as yet another sign of her submission.

Lady Smythe knew that this girl continued to crave a good spanking at least occasionally so as to relive that excitement that she had first encountered as a child. She would spank the girl for her own good as well as for her own pleasure then they she would introduce her friend to the delights of actually inflicting exquisite pain.

As she raised the hem of Lucinda's dress Lady Smythe drank in the beautiful sight of the girl's long coltish legs clad in those cream stockings that were so very difficult to get hold of in wartime. They were held up by garters decorated with pretty blue bows which circled her thighs and perfectly complemented the cornflower blue of her charming dress.

This girl obviously had style even when her husband was away but Lady Smythe took a sharp intake of breath when she pulled the skirt over Lucinda's firm buttocks. She was shocked because beneath her dress and delicate lace petticoat Lucinda was naked.

"What's wrong, Miss?" asked Lucinda, worried that she had somehow offended her chastiser further.

"You are not wearing anything under your skirts," said Lady Smythe incredulously.

"It gets far too hot during the day," offered Lucinda meekly.

"I know my dear, but all the same, you should..."

"I know and I am sorry," said a shamed Lucinda. "Perhaps you should increase my punishment?"

"Yes, I think I better had," said Lady Smythe almost joyfully. "A young lady should never be seen in public with out proper undergarments, however hot the weather!"

Lady Smythe was absolutely delighted at the prospect spanking this lovely creature even more than she had initially planned to. She had been right about this girl wanting to be punished by a figure of authority in her life but Lady Smythe also knew that she would take to having the whip hand as well.

"Now I am going to spank you as hard as I can for you have been a very naughty girl," warned Lady Smythe. "And, when I have finished you will kneel at my feet and thank me for putting you back on the straight and narrow, do you understand?"

"Yes, Miss, thank you, Miss," responded Lucinda hoping that her friend wouldn't be too hard on her.

She felt very vulnerable over Lady Smythe's knee but she couldn't help feeling thoroughly excited also at the prospect of having her bottom smacked by this woman's firm hand. She wriggled her bottom as if to draw attention to Lady Smythe's target and to spur her into action.

"Well, young lady, let's get started and remember that this will hurt me as much as it hurts you," lied Lady Smythe as she raised her arm high above her head.

With as much force as she could muster Lady Smythe brought the palm of her hand down onto Lucinda's creamy white cheeks with a loud slap. Immediately she felt her hand tingle with the aftershock of the blow but most of the energy of her first spank had been transferred to the soft flesh of Lucinda's pert buttocks.

As she lifted up her arm to continue the punishment Lady Smythe was satisfied to see a large red handprint appearing across Lucinda's bottom. She could also hear Lucinda sigh as she absorbed the pain that was spreading through her nether regions. There would be a lot more of that before Lady Smythe was finished with her plus many more bright red hand prints.

Once more Lady Smythe brought her hand down to deliver another stinging smack to Lucinda's proffered backside making her victim moan quietly in agony. Lady Smythe was really enjoying herself but she had to make sure that she strung the punishment out as long as she could so as to glean maximum enjoyment from it.

Lady Smythe spanked Lucinda again with even more force than the first two but swiftly followed this by stroking her reddened buttocks as tenderly as she could.

"There, there, my dear," she crooned to the already snivelling Lucinda. "You are doing very well so far."

"Thank you, Miss," sniffed Lucinda, struggling to cope with the smarting in her bottom. She was surprised that Lady Smythe could bring about so much suffering from only three spanks.

When Lady Smythe started again with her first slap Lucinda heard herself cry out with the shock. She had really enjoyed the gentle caresses from Lady Smythe's surprisingly soft fingers as they danced over her burning skin.

Now she had to endure more scalding slaps as they rained down on her defenceless buttocks. Her head began to spin as the pain seemed to shudder through her entire body but she remained resolutely where she was, determined to prove to her tormentor that she could take punishment.

It had been just like this all those years ago when her father had brought tears to her eyes with his relentlessly hard hand or whip. She had cried in misery as a little girl but those other feelings that left her all excited and confused were the same as those she was experiencing now under Lady Smythe's hand.

As her bottom began to glow like a beacon Lucinda started to sense that churning between her legs that she had been forced to deal with as a teenager. Her nipples were rock hard again making her realise that she was being aroused by this constant attack on her buttocks.

She was desperate to go away and relieve herself but still Lady Smythe's hand flashed down to deliver yet more agony to her quivering form.

"That will do for now," announced Lady Smythe suddenly, rubbing Lucinda's bottom sensitively after her last slap.

Her hand was hurting for it was a long time since she had spanked anybody. She was happier to use instruments of correction other than her hands these days but she also sensed that her prey had already had enough for the moment.

"Thank you, Miss," said Lucinda, sliding from Lady Smythe's thighs and onto her knees before her.

Lucinda took hold of Lady Smythe's hands in order to cover them with kisses as a sign of her gratitude. Her bottom hurt like the devil but she was as aroused as she could ever remember. All she wanted to do was to trot off and find a discreet place in which to play with herself.

"You want to go now don't you, young lady?" enquired

Lady Smythe knowingly.

"Yes, Miss...if that's alright Miss," replied Lucinda sheepishly.

"You want to play with yourself, don't you?" asked Lady Smythe with a mischievous edge in her voice.

"How do...yes, Miss," muttered Lucinda, mortified that her intentions were fully understood by her all-knowing friend.

"Why don't you let me help you, as I have done already by spanking you?" suggested Lady playfully.

"But I couldn't possibly..." pleaded Lucinda.

She was disturbed by how much she really wanted Lady Smythe to play with her helpless body. There was nothing she wanted more at that moment than to have her former tormentor turn into her lover, treating her to entirely different kinds of strokes.

"I think that you could," insisted Lady Smythe. "In fact I know that you want me to."

"No, we shouldn't," begged Lucinda feebly. "What about my husband?"

"He is isn't here, is he?" Lady Smythe said urgently grabbing Lucinda's shoulders in order to pull her forward. In one swift movement she darted forward to kiss her young friend passionately on her ruby lips. Without any compunction she forced her tongue between Lucinda's lips and deep into her mouth.

Lucinda tried to pull away but Lady Smythe had much too firm a grip on her and she had no choice other than to join in. She responded with her own tongue in a way that she had so rarely done with her husband as the pounding passion rose within her. Within moments their arms were wrapped around each other in an ardent embrace as they explored their bodies together. Their hands strayed over forbidden flesh in an attempt to seek further stimulation of their already excited bodies.

It wasn't long before they were rolling around on the veranda moaning with lust, driving one another on to inevitable orgasms. Clothes were shed in a blizzard of material leaving their owners naked and accessible for even closer investigation by the other. Lips closed in on exposed nipples whilst fingers probed sodden pussies as their moans of pleasure rose in a highly charged crescendo. These groans became cries of delight as they both came together, their bodies quivering with the endless aftershocks of their shattering orgasms.

"We shouldn't have done that," murmured Lucinda guiltily as they lay recovering on the cool, tiled floor.

"Why on earth not?" Lady Smythe said easily, dropping an affirming kiss on her young lover's forehead.

"Our husbands would be mortified if they were to find out," insisted Lucinda.

"Well, they're not going to," Lady Smythe assured her. "Although I am sure that the Colonel would be fascinated to know what we've been up to."

"You wouldn't tell him, would you?" Lucinda asked, horrified at the prospect of their activities being discovered.

"That would rather depend on whether you were going to be a good girl from now on, wouldn't it?"

"What do you mean?" asked Lucinda nervously.

"I mean that you will have to come to visit me every day from now on as well as behaving yourself at all times," explained Lady Smythe. "The alternative is of course, severe punishment or even a word with the Colonel."

"Oh no, don't do that, I will do as you say and behave, I promise," stammered Lucinda desperate to keep their secret hidden.

And so began a relationship between the two women that was to take them both on a journey of pure pain and pleasure with Lady Smythe leading her young charge every step of the way. She continued to share her stories but they were increasingly embellished with 'hands on' experiences that Lucinda was eager to undergo.

Most of the time a hard spanking sufficed for the naughty little girl but occasionally, for really bad offences or when Lucinda had been very disobedient Lady Smythe was forced to use the crop that she normally reserved only for her horse. The long white switch, made of supple ash with a beautifully carved handle always struck terror into the heart of poor Lucinda but she always too, submitted meekly to it. In the hands of her new mistress it was a most unnerving instrument of correction but the agony that it produced for her was far better than Colonel Smythe finding out what she did with Lady Smythe.

As the weeks passed Lucinda found that she could take increasing amounts of punishment before begging for mercy. She also discovered new dimensions to the eroticism of being chastised by a powerful and authoritative figure.

Lady Smythe took her to places where she was reluctant to go but the fact that she had no choice other than to obey made the adventures even more delicious. The anguish that these trips usually produced was always eclipsed by the ecstasy that quickly followed.

She was even made to serve between her mistress's legs as what Lady Smythe liked to refer to as her little pet. At first she thought it was a pretty disgusting idea but she rapidly got used to the taste of excited sex as she lapped away merrily on her friend's pussy. Lady Smythe would recline on her chaise longue with no underwear on as well as the hem of her dress pulled up to her waist. Lucinda would then be ordered to kneel before her in order to lick her to slow satisfying orgasms until she decided that she could come no more.

If she was pleased with Lucinda's performance between her thighs then Lady Smythe treated her to an orgasm by fingering her soaking pussy. But if she was not immediately persuaded of Lucinda's commitment to her task then no matter how many orgasms Lady Smythe attained poor Lucinda would be beaten for her slovenliness.

All in all Lady Smythe felt that the initiation of this impressionable girl into the ways of submission was going very well. Lucinda was responding well to the discipline as well as the conditioning but the time had now come to take the chastisements to the next level - it was time for the triangle.

"Lucinda, you are simply not trying hard enough!" Lady Smythe told her slavegirl as she attempted yet again to please her mistress with her tongue.

"I am sorry, mistress," replied Lucinda lapping vigorously between Lady Smythe's parted labia.

Her bottom was already sore from the preliminary spanking that Lady Smythe had given her for a minor infringement of her ever-growing list of rules. Lucinda knew only too well that failure to please between her mistress's legs would lead to more severe punishments.

Lucinda's mouth was already filled with juices from Lady Smythe's pussy betraying the fact that her mistress had already come many times. But this was obviously not enough for her hard taskmistress because she stood up with a stern look on her face clearly intending some further correction for what she regarded as her lazy vassal.

"Come with me, little girl, for your behaviour has proved to me that you are in need of a more severe form of punishment," she announced haughtily.

"Yes, Mistress," said Lucinda miserably, following her mistress.

Lady Smythe led her through to a small open air courtyard that she had never seen before at the rear of the house. In the centre of the yard, surrounded by flowering blossom trees

Lucinda was deeply shocked to see a triangular frame that resembled the contraption described by Lady Smythe so many times in her stories of India.

"This was made by the Colonel out of lances taken from the French after the British Army took Madrid last year," explained Lady Smythe airily. "The Colonel decided that we should have one here for our personal use."

"Yes, Mistress," said Lucinda, wondering what she meant by 'our personal use'.

"I have been building you up to this moment gradually, but now it appears that you are more than ready for it," continued Lady Smythe. "Remove your dress and go over to the frame so that I may prepare you for your first meeting with the whip," ordered Lady Smythe.

"Yes, Mistress," mumbled Lucinda.

She let her dress fall to the floor before raising her arms and spreading her legs within in the 'A' of the pike frame.

"Very good, Lucinda, you have obviously been listening carefully to my stories," said a pleased Lady Smythe as she proceeded to tie her slave's wrist and ankles to the frame. "Perhaps I won't give you quite as many strokes as I had planned after all."

"Thank you, Mistress, I am very grateful," breathed Lucinda nervously.

Once Lady Smythe had secured Lucinda to the frame in proper military fashion she went to retrieve the fearful whip leaving Lucinda to ponder her situation. She could feel the warmth of the sun on her back and smell the blossom in the air but nothing could take her mind off the dreaded flogging to come.

Lady Smythe's arrival with the whip did nothing to soothe Lucinda for she brandished the multi-tailed instrument of torture under her victim's nose. She wanted her prey to see what would bring the explosions of pain across her back before she took up her position behind her.

"I will give you ten, so you have an idea of what an army flogging feels like, do you understand?" Lady Smythe said, swishing the whip through the air menacingly. "First, however, there is the bit which, as you can see, I am preparing so you have something nice to bite on as I flog you."

"Thank you, Mistress," said Lucinda looking over her shoulder.

Sure enough she could see that her mistress had lifted up her skirts in order to rub the wooden bit between the still wet lips of her sex. Lucinda's belly churned with a blend of fear and excitement as she thought of Lady Smythe strapping the tainted device in her mouth before she was whipped.

When she was sure that the bit was wet enough she placed it between Lucinda's teeth then bound it tightly at the back of her neck with the attached straps. A couple of steps backward took her to her position where she wasted no time in raising the whip above her shoulder.

Not even the weeks of careful nurturing could prepare poor Lucinda for the anguish of the first stroke that Lady Smythe mercilessly delivered. The resounding crack of the whip released a torrent of pain across Lucinda's exposed back that caused her to pull uselessly at her bonds. She screamed loudly as she pulled against the coarse rope that held her in that painful frame but all her efforts to escape the flogging were in vain. Lady Smythe had bound her so well that there was no way for her to avoid the scalding lashes.

Lucinda tried to beg her friend to cease this tirade against her but the gag, which had brought a wonderful taste sensation to her mouth a moment before, thwarted her. She could only cry out in pain for she was totally incapable of forming any words to plead with her tormentor.

Another stroke caught Lucinda between her straining shoulder blades bringing another bout of anguish to her racked form. She attempted to look over her shoulder in sheer desperation but all she could see was a woman supremely focused on dishing out the allotted punishment.

In fact Lady Smythe was enjoying herself immensely as she slashed the whip across her friend's helpless buttocks with her third stroke. There was a limit to the number of strokes this girl could take and she didn't want to push her too far on her first visit to the frame. Ten would have to be enough for the moment so she would happily savour every lash each time she brought the whip savagely down over Lucinda's beautiful body.

Even though Lucinda was lost in the haze of mounting pain she began to wonder whether her back was beginning to resemble a tiger. Every stroke, she surmised, must have deposited a regiment of fearful red lines over her skin, but this thought was only a temporary distraction from the seemingly endless onslaught on her body.

But for Lady Smythe the end came too soon for she reached her tenth stroke all too quickly for her liking. Still, she had to be fair on the poor girl but she made sure that the final stroke was one that Lucinda would certainly remember.

With a terrifying snap she brought the whip down on Lucinda's back with all her strength, causing her victim to jerk forward violently. Lady Smythe sighed with deep satisfaction as the concluding whip marks burned their way into the glowing flesh of Lucinda's back.

For her part Lucinda screamed as loudly as she could into her gag for the pain that spread across her lower back was absolutely excruciating. It was beyond anything that she thought she could bear but bear it she had to as she pulled vainly on her ropes.

"Hush now, baby, it is all over," said Lady Smythe soothingly.

She walked round to the front of the frame in order to take Lucinda's tear-stained face gently in her hands. She had done so well but she could not give her a congratulatory hug for fear of adding to the agony over her scarlet-striped back.

A swift kiss on her blushing cheeks sufficed before she left Lucinda to contemplate her punishment in her bonds for a while.

When Lucinda looked over her shoulder she could not believe that her mistress was walking away without releasing her from her stringent bondage. She couldn't understand how she could do this to her after she had been so utterly merciless to her with the whip. To her it felt like hours of waiting as she continued to struggle against the ropes that held her so firmly. Her back was still ablaze with the pain from her flogging and her limbs were aching from the tautness of her enforced stance. She wanted to be released so that her mistress could comfort her but Lady Smythe strung out the suspense as long as she could.

Eventually she returned to release her victim who immediately fell to her feet in grovelling gratitude. Lady Smythe may have been mean to her but Lucinda was determined to thank her for her punishment as well as to show her mistress how pleased she was to have been released from the frame.

"There's a good girl," gushed Lady Smythe, so pleased at her slave girl's reaction to release. "It looks like I have taught you well, doesn't it?"

"Yes, Mistress," replied Lucinda as humbly as she could.

"Now you know what happens to soldiers when they are bad," explained Lady Smythe. "If you are naughty again then you might end up tied to the frame once more!"

"Yes, Mistress," whispered Lucinda, terrified at the prospect of receiving another flogging at the hands of her mistress.

She fully intended to behave so well that Lady Smythe couldn't find any cause to flog her. Every time the two friends met Lucinda tried her very best to behave well but Lady Smythe always found some way to trick her or catch her being a naughty girl. Then punishment would inevitably follow with Lady Smythe deciding the magnitude of the crime as well as the severity of the chastisement that had been earned. Sometimes Lucinda would be hauled over her mistress's knee but other times she found herself strapped to the dreaded frame and awaiting another flogging.

Whichever punishment Lady Smythe chose Lucinda was always left with a very sore bottom and promises to herself that she would behave better in future. These promises were seldom kept but there were the benefits that followed in the form of a good spanking or a hard flogging.

Lady Smythe always comforted her after a beating which usually led to energetic and joyous lovemaking between the pair of them. Very severe chastisements meant that Lucinda was allowed to stay with her mistress so that she could be comforted all night.

This led to the unusual situation for Lucinda whereby she feared the punishments meted out by Lady Smythe but she really craved hard beatings so that she could enjoy the pleasures of her mistress's bed. The harder her mistress beat her the more fun Lucinda would have afterwards but she found some of the floggings hard to take.

Sometimes Lady Smythe would simply point to the passageway through to the dreaded courtyard expecting her slavegirl to go through without being ordered. Occasionally one of Lady Smythe's maids would bind Lucinda to her frame of pain if the mistress of the house couldn't be bothered. This was particularly embarrassing for Lucinda for it was made clear to her that the servants of the household all knew what was going on. Being tied by a maid of lower class than herself added to the humiliation.

Lucinda tried to prepare herself for her floggings as best she could when she was sent through the dark passageways to her fate. But she was not prepared for what she saw when she was sent through one day for some unspecified misdemeanour. When she reached the frame there was already somebody bound to it - a man.

At first Lucinda was shocked but this turned to disbelief when she finally realised who the man with his back to her was. Even though he was blindfolded with a colourful scarf and was gagged with the heavy wooden bit Lucinda recognised the man. For tied to the frame in the same way as she had been many times before was none other than the Colonel himself.

He was completely naked with the afternoon sun glaring down on his still lily-white back. Lucinda could see perspiration glistening on his skin which made her think that he had been waiting some considerable time in the heat of the day.

"Isn't he magnificent?" whispered Lady Smythe.

"Yes, Mistress," stammered Lucinda. "But what on earth is he doing there?"

"He is back from the fighting for a few days," answered Lady Smythe, playfully avoiding the point of Lucinda's astonished question.

"But why is he in my place?" asked a bewildered Lucinda who was by now so used to being strung up between the pikes.

"Well, it's a long story..."

Lady Smythe went on to explain that ever since he had seen her flog the soldier in India the Colonel had insisted that his wife flog him occasionally. In accordance with military law he also insisted that he be bound as a soldier would be between the pikes.

This had been going on for years, especially after the

Colonel's return from long periods away from his domineering wife. He would be bound as he was now and left to wait for his punishment so that his excitement before the flogging could be built up to fever pitch.

"So this is the state he is in now," continued Lady Smythe in a low voice. "Look you can see his willy is already huge!"

Lucinda blushed as her eyes were drawn to what was a truly magnificent erection, much bigger than she remembered her husband's to be. The colonel's member was simply enormous and she even experienced a stab of envy as she gazed at it.

"Now I suppose you are wondering why I shared this with you," continued Lady Smythe almost under her breath.

"Yes, Mistress, I was," replied Lucinda also wondering why they were both whispering.

"I want you find out what it feels like to flog a man," said Lady Smythe simply.

"But I..."

"No 'buts'," interrupted Lady Smythe forcefully. "I set out to introduce you to the world of pain and pleasure - now is the time for you to discover the delights of handing out a severe flogging."

"What if he..."

"He won't know that you're here, as long as you don't speak," insisted Lady Smythe. "He'll think it was me all along!"

Reluctantly Lucinda took the whip that had so often caused her to cry in agony and approached the defenceless Colonel. His firm buttocks jutted out behind him presenting an all too tempting target for Lucinda's newly acquired lash.

"Now Colonel, you've been a very naughty boy so it's time for a severe beating for you, my boy," said Lady Smythe in a loud patronising voice. "I think that I will give you twenty five this time for you have been very naughty indeed!"

The Colonel stiffened in his bonds at the sound of his wife's stern voice but no sound came from his bitted mouth. Lucinda looked round at her friend for confirmation that she should go ahead with the beating but Lady Smythe only nodded her assent. Slowly Lucinda raised the whip above her shoulder. With a resounding crack she launched the first satisfying stroke against the Colonel's unprotected back and he groaned loudly into his gag. As the first set of vivid red stripes started to appear between the Colonel's shoulders Lucinda lifted the whip once more. She could feel excitement building up within her, a different kind of excitement to the sort that she experienced when being whipped herself. This thrill came from having power over another person, of having them at her mercy and helpless. Again she brought the whip down this time on the lower part of the Colonel's back but it didn't matter to her where the whip fell. She wanted to flog this man as hard as she could for she was enjoying every second of it.

Her right arm became a blur as she started to land blows indiscriminately all over the poor Colonel's back. Meanwhile her other hand strayed between her own legs for she had the overwhelming desire to play with herself as she flogged away.

As the lashing continued to mark the Colonel's skin Lucinda lifted her skirts so that she could finger her naked sex. Her lips were already wet so it was easy for her to slip a couple of probing fingers up into her sodden vagina.

With the whip flailing away in front of her she rammed her fingers in and out of her pussy as quickly as she could. Her moans of pleasure soon mingled with the Colonel's gargled cries of pain as they echoed around the whitewashed walls of the courtyard. Lucinda laid on stroke after stroke on the Colonel's back as well as on her own sex until she felt her first orgasm fast approaching. With each successive blow of the whip the millions of bubbles of excitement grew within her before they burst wonderfully between her legs. Her body shook as she came to send judders ripping through her entire body but this did not put her off her stride. As she continued to whip away her body was racked with aftershocks from her first climax as well as the rumblings of fresh orgasms building in her belly.

When she delivered the last stroke upon the mass of crimson weals that covered the Colonel's back she came one last time with as much force as all the other orgasms put together. She was lucky that her abandoned cry of delight was drowned by the Colonel's concluding scream of anguish.

All Lucinda could do once the flogging was over was stand and regain her breath for she had put everything into punishing the Colonel. She wasn't even embarrassed that she had used the opportunity to play with herself because she had done a good job for which she was simply rewarding herself.

They left the Colonel to suffer a little longer once Lucinda had composed herself, deciding to go back to the veranda in the shade.

"You did well, my dear," said Lady Smythe warmly. "Did you enjoy yourself?"

"Yes, Mistress, thank you so much," replied Lucinda quickly.

"Well, it is for you to decide who is mistress now," said Lady Smythe.

"What do you mean?"

"Your husband is waiting for you in your apartment," continued Lady Smythe. "I suggest you make up your mind on your journey to him which of you will hold the whip hand!"

Lucinda understood immediately that Lady Smythe had been training her for the rest of her marriage but she had to decide before she was reunited with her gallant captain.

She hugged Lady Smythe warmly then wandered out into the street towards her house near the centre of the city. As she walked she could not decide whether she would prefer to submit to her husband or have him at her feet.

It was only when she reached her large oak door that she realised that she still had the whip she had used on the Colonel in her hand. Her mind was finally made up so she climbed the grand staircase towards her Captain and her new life in a dominant role.

When the drum roll ended the only sounds that could be heard were the creaking of timbers and the splashing of waves against the sides of the ship. The men were quiet for although they enjoyed the spectacle of a flogging as much as the next man they knew that Miranda wanted absolute silence.

"Now you dogs, I am going to remind you why I am in charge of this ship and not any of you scum," shouted Miranda, tossing her long blonde hair in disgust at her crew.

She was a tall statuesque woman with all the authority of an old sea captain added to the beauty of an English rose. Her face was set in an angry grimace as she considered the task ahead of her but her scowl could not hide her attractive features. Her dark green eyes set above high cheek bones were offset by her full ruby lips through which so many harsh orders had passed. Her yellow hair framed her face perfectly when allowed to fall to her shoulders although on deck she often wore a ponytail to keep strands of hair from blowing into her eyes.

Her long legs were encased in tight, cream coloured breeches as well as thigh length boots of highly polished black leather. A crisp white blouse bedecked with flamboyant frills completed her outfit, which was laced up only just enough to prevent her magnificent breasts from spilling out.

In her hand she held a long dark brown bullwhip, which trailed on the floor beside her like a venomous snake. She looked around her crew with contempt to ensure that she had their complete attention for what she was about to do.

"I am going to flog this son of a sea slug to within an inch of his life to teach him, and you lot, a lesson you won't forget," she stated, pointing the wooden handle of her scourge towards the intended victim of her anger.

The unfortunate man had been strung up from the lower yardarm of the central mast of the large ship, which had formerly been the frigate San Juan of the Royal Spanish Navy. It had been captured by its present crew from the Spanish in 1710 and had been operated as a pirate vessel under the name of Miranda's Revenge ever since.

Bates hung in his bonds several feet above the deck as he waited for the wrath of his captain descended upon his naked torso. He was quite clearly terrified of the prospect of being beaten by this woman because this was no ordinary woman.

Miranda, the self-proclaimed captain of Miranda's Revenge ruled her crew with a rod of iron. It was not uncommon for a man to pass out several times during the course of one of her punishments for she was a fearful expert with her infamous whip.

Now she stood in the midst of her company with Bates totally at her mercy as an example as well as a reminder of her authority over her rag-bag crew. He had dared to defy her so he would be made to pay. She needed to reassert herself of the rabble before they got any ideas about ousting her.

Miranda had taken the ship from Johnson, its previous captain in an armed uprising but she knew that she had to keep fighting in order to remain in charge. She made sure that the crew had a plentiful supply of ships to plunder and fine women to ravish.

She had been a good captain so far so the crew had put up with her but occasionally men like Bates decided that they would challenge her command. She usually came down on them like a ton of bricks and this time would be no exception for she was really going to let Bates have it.

"Be warned that any one else who crosses me will get this and more!" she yelled, looking round at the expectant faces.

She realised that the men also liked to watch her as she administered the punishments for she knew that she had an extremely sexy body, especially whilst whipping her naughty boys. She revelled in the attention that she got when flogging her victims, which added to her enjoyment of the occasions.

Once she was satisfied that everyone was watching her she stood behind Bates with her whip hand high in the air. Without any further warning she slashed the long whip down across Bates's back with an ear splitting snap.

His scream rivalled the cries of the ever-hungry seagulls that seemed to follow the ship whenever they were near to land. The first blow must have hurt him a lot but Miranda smiled for she knew his comrades would think him a wimp for giving in to shrieking at the first stroke.

She knew immediately that she had won her men back already but she wanted to continue enjoying herself for a while at Bates's expense. She brought the whip down so hard the second time that Bates was made to dance in the air like a helpless marionette. Miranda was laughing as she struck her prey a third time for Bates was whimpering like a baby with tears rolling down his face. He was begging her to stop but she would not until she was certain that all her men had witnessed her fully regaining the ascendancy on deck.

Another blow with Miranda's whip sent Bates swinging forward in his cradle of agony but his high-pitched screaming did not put his tormentor off her aim. Two more strokes followed in quick succession before she was satisfied that she had made her point in front of her men.

"Don't cut that down until I give the order," she announced as she turned to walk off towards her cabin. "I want him to hang there so he can think about what he's done!"

Miranda was anxious to get back to the relative privacy of her cabin because the flogging had aroused the passion deep within her. She could see that her nipples were already poking their way through her blouse as she stalked off and she knew that she would be wet between her legs.

As she burst through the door of her cabin she saw that her cabin boy was kneeling in the corner facing the wood panelling where she had left him a few hours before. He had spilled some wine onto her earlier in the day so she had placed him there as a prelude to his punishment later on.

"So, you're still here are you, you snivelling wretch?" she said scornfully.

"Yes, Mistress," replied the boy miserably in a thick French accent.

"Well we'd better sort your punishment out as well, hadn't we?" continued Miranda mercilessly.

"Yes, Mistress, we had," he conceded disconsolately.

"Get over here then and we'll get started," ordered Miranda, delighted at Jean's compliance.

The boy quickly scuttled over to where his mistress stood with her lags splayed apart and her hands on her hips. He did not want to upset this woman any more than he already had for she had already beaten him many times, even in front of her men.

He had been serving Miranda for three months ever since his capture from a French Corvette during a skirmish with Miranda's Revenge. He had been a Top Mast Man in the French Navy but because he was the youngest of the French crew at barely eighteen years old Miranda had selected him to be her cabin boy.

His duties had been very wide ranging since his capture, from helping his mistress to bathe to serving her food. There had also been other duties to perform in Miranda's hard narrow bed but somehow he knew that his bad behaviour would lead to pain for him instead of that particular pleasure.

107

"Fetch the low stool because I would like to sit down after all my exertions outside," demanded Miranda.

Jean quickly obeyed knowing exactly what this would mean for him because Miranda had ordered the stool many times before. After placing it in the centre of the small cabin he stripped off the few clothes his mistress allowed him to wear to reveal a taut muscular body.

Once he was naked he knelt down with his back to the stool holding his ankles solidly with his hands. Carefully he put his head back onto the seat, which meant that his already hardening penis was thrust out in front of him.

Miranda watched his every trained move with hawk-like eyes drinking in the view of Jean's magnificent cock as she imagined being impaled upon his firm flesh. But first she would sit down to rest as she dreamt up what she would do to the boy before she used his member for her own pleasure again.

Thoughtfully Miranda straddled the stool facing his wonderful prick before lowering herself gently onto Jean's upturned face. She wiggled her bottom slightly so that she could feel his nose sticking up between the cheeks of her bottom for she knew that he could smell her arousal even through her britches.

As she was still holding her whip Miranda began to trail its leathery lash up his flat stomach causing him to shiver beneath her. Skilfully she coiled the end of her long whip around the base of his rampant cock then pulled the plaited leather back towards her. Out of sheer devilment she decided to loop the lash around the base of Jean's cock and balls about half way along the length of the whip. Then, taking both ends of the lash she pulled outwards thus applying greater pressure to that most sensitive area

Jean moaned softly as he struggled for breath but he could not deny that, despite the pain he was highly aroused by this kind of treatment. He felt the lash tugging relentlessly at his

108

cock which made him even more excited. He longed to take hold of his penis so that he could relieve the pressure building up in his loins but he dare not even let go of his ankles without his Miranda's permission. The cabin boy would have to wait on his mistress's pleasure before he was allowed any himself.

"So what do you think I should do to you for spilling my wine, boy?" Asked Miranda knowing full well that that Jean couldn't reply.

"What, too ashamed to offer any suggestions?" continued Miranda, ignoring Jean's muffled attempts to reply. "Well, I think that you should help me play with myself and then I might put you in my locker for the night; what do you think?"

Once more Jean tried to respond but Miranda simply pressed further down on his face with her bottom. She did not want him to reply just to serve so it rarely suited her purposes for her slave boy to answer her back. Tormenting him with rhetorical questions was all part of Jean's training and denying the boy the right to speak was essential.

"Come, help me get undressed, boy then we'll see if you are any better with that tongue of yours," said Miranda standing up from her human perch.

Jean scrambled to his feet so that he could follow her over to her bed whereupon he fell to his knees. As she sat on her bunk Jean began to remove her thigh length boots after first lifting each one so he could kiss the sole. Lovingly he pulled off Miranda's boots before moving up her body to take off her blouse. He untied the knot that held the straining laces together so that his mistress's beautiful breasts fell out practically smothering him.

Because he was not allowed to touch them without permission he moved back in order to remove the blouse leaving the top half of Miranda's body naked. Jean noticed that her rouged nipples were rock hard but his staring was curtailed as

109

she stood up in front of him.

"Time to take the britches off, I think," she announced with her hands on her hips.

Jean leaned forward so that he could untie the laces that held Miranda's britches up with his teeth. Even though he successfully undid the knot he was not surprised to see that the pants would not slide down by themselves for they were far too tight for that.

Instead he had to use his teeth again to drag them down over her full thighs and buttocks until they finally dropped to the floor at her feet. Once there he bent down to retrieve them so that he could offer them to his mistress like a good dog.

"There's a good boy," said Miranda patronisingly as she patted Jean's head. "Now put them by my locker then come back to service your mistress."

By the time Jean had scurried away to obey Miranda had laid back in her bed with her long legs parted invitingly. He could see her beauty lips peeping out from the hair at the top of her thighs, they were already glistening with her juices.

Jean did not need to be told what to do for his mistress had thoroughly schooled him in the ways of pleasuring her. He mounted the narrow bed with his hands grasped behind his back as he had been taught and ducked down between her thighs. He had been able to smell Miranda's arousal through her pants but now the rich aroma of her sex filled his nostrils. Jean wasted no time in adding taste to smell as he licked along the gaping red gash nestled in the midst of his mistress's black pubic hair.

After a few long laps with Jean's expert tongue Miranda began to moan loudly as waves of delight began to crash over her. She had taught the boy well so all she had to do was lie back and enjoy his expert attention. She pulled her stiff nipples as Jean worked away between her thighs so that she could

110

heighten her sensual pleasure even more. She knew exactly how much pressure to apply in order to gain maximum satisfaction from the pain she created.

Miranda had become an expert in dishing out pain to the extent that she was aware precisely how much anguish each of her crew could take. This included Lola the charming little Danish maid who cooked and tasted all Miranda's meals for her.

Whilst Jean drove her towards her first orgasm Miranda thought about the last time she had spanked poor Lola. She had spilled some soup in a storm but Miranda had ignored her mitigating pleas for mercy as she hauled the young blonde over her knee for a bare bottomed spanking. The girl had squealed as she was punished, as much in pleasure as in pain, for she loved to be near her mistress almost as much as Jean did. Perhaps one day Miranda would put the two young things together to see what would happen, under her personal guidance of course.

The thought of whipping her two personal galley slaves into shape sent her emotions over the edge as her first orgasm blasted through her courtesy of Jeans skilful tongue. As she swam in her own sea of delights she grabbed Jean's hair in order to encourage him towards further effort with his tongue.

Whilst Jean continued with his endeavours on her behalf Miranda turned her thoughts to her crew and how she would keep them in shape as well as on her side. They were a tough lot and if she didn't keep them completely satisfied they could all quite easily turn against her.

Lola and Jean were strictly off limits to the rest of the crew so all they had to go at between them were the two black girls who were kept in the hold of the ship. Miranda's Revenge had come across the two runaway slaves during a raid on one of the smaller Caribbean islands whereupon they had been taken prisoner for use by the crew.

They were held in almost permanent bondage as well as in semi-darkness and had learnt that the arrival of light meant more sexual acts that they were required to perform. Whichever crewmember had drawn the lucky straw was allowed down to the hold to choose his favourite slave to use or abuse to his heart's content. The poor girls had been raped in all conceivable positions by every member of the crew at least twice since their capture to the extent that they wished they had never run away. Their pussies were permanently sore from constant use and all they could taste was the semen that had been regularly deposited in their mouths since their ordeal had begun. Miranda knew that the men enjoyed the use of the girls but they often fought amongst themselves if they didn't pick the right straw. She realised that as their leader she would have to provide more entertainment for them soon so she decided to sleep on it alone in the hope of dreaming up a solution.

"That's enough, boy," she announced, pushing Jean away from her dripping sex. "Now go and get in your box like a good little boy."

"But Mistress..."

"No buts," insisted Miranda forcefully. "I need to think so do as you're told or I will really punish you!"

"Yes, Mistress," said Jean scrambling away to the chest in the corner of the room.

Without another word he climbed into the wooden box, curling himself up into a ball so that he could fit in. He pulled the lid down with a loud bang signifying his total submission to his mistress who deigned to stroll over in order to lock him in with a heavy padlock. She was pleased to be rid of his distracting presence for the moment as she tried to think, although she smiled as she heard him struggling inside the box. Miranda knew that he was trying to play with his erect cock within the

112

confines of the box. She laughed to herself as she heard the distant dull thudding of his frantic activity in dark cramped container. Miranda knew that she should open the box in order to punish him severely but she was secretly pleased that he was so turned on by serving her that he felt he had to risk serious chastisement to relieve his excitement.

Miranda decided to leave him to it but she vowed to make him lick up any traces of his seemingly imminent orgasm first thing in the morning. First she needed sleep so that she could clearly think about how to keep her crew amused in the morning. After blowing out the ornate oil lamp by her bed she lay back and prepared herself for sleep, her mind filled with fretful images from her recent past. Visions of what had happened to her before she took over Miranda's Revenge raced through her head, times and places that she longed to forget.

She awoke before dawn in a cold sweat desperately trying to reassure herself that she was still in charge of the ship. Miranda certainly did not want to return to the life she had endured in the months before she teamed up with the crew of the Miranda. Instead she would ensure that her crew were happy with her, especially her little toy locked up in his box. She slid out of her bed still naked so that she could release her plaything as well as check on the presence of any overnight issue from his overexcited cock.

"Now then, what have you been up to, young man?" said Miranda patronisingly as Jean struggled to get out of the chest.

"Nothing, Mistress," Jean replied nervously.

"What's this then?" she demanded staring at a white sticky residue on the inside of the box.

"Well, I er..."

"You have been a naughty boy, haven't you?" continued Miranda. "You know that I am going to have to make you pay."

"Yes, Mistress; sorry Mistress," stammered the boy falling

113

to his knees with terror in his eyes.

"I will give you a choice of chastisements for playing with yourself without permission," said Miranda firmly. "We could make Lola lick it up whilst I spank you with my paddle or you can lick it out yourself, the choice is yours."

"Please Mistress, make Lola do it whist you beat me," begged Jean.

He had been made to lap up his own semen when he had accidentally come all over his mistress's breasts. He had of course enjoyed running his tongue over her firm nipples but the taste of his own issue was something that he wanted to avoid. Let the maid lick it up and he would take his chances with the paddle.

"Fetch her then and don't bother with any clothes for either of you," ordered Miranda much to his embarrassment.

He ran from the cabin with his cock already stiffening in the early morning chill towards the tiny room where Lola was allowed to sleep. He found her fast asleep curled up at the bottom of the broom cupboard surrounded by deck mops.

"Lola, wake up, the mistress wants you," urged Jean rousing her from her slumbers.

Both naked apart from the tiny apron that was permanently tied around Lola's waist they both ran off to Miranda's cabin hoping that nobody had seen them.

"Come in," called Miranda upon hearing Jean's timid knock on her door.

"Ah there you are, little Lola, " she said admiring her buxom maid's body. "Jean has left something for you to clean up whilst I give him a damn good thrashing for being such a naughty boy."

"Yes, Mistress," said Lola walking over to the toy box where Miranda indicated the dirty deed had taken place with the paddle already in her hand.

"And you, young man, can get here and place yourself over my knee like the rogue you are!" Miranda ordered the cowering Jean.

Having no choice in the matter as he had decided upon punishment rather than the humiliation of cleaning his box Jean draped his quivering body over his mistress' thighs. He knew that Miranda would pummel him with her paddle as hard as she could at least until Lola had lapped up his mess.

For her part Lola was quite relieved at only having to lean over the side of the chest in order to lick its smooth interior. She liked the taste of semen although she preferred it warm and freshly spurting deep into her mouth from some strapping man's cock end.

As she bent over Lola made sure that her mistress could see her shapely legs which she spread invitingly as she struggled to reach Jean's issue. She knew that Miranda liked to see between her slave girl's legs especially when she was chastising another of her slaves.

"That's a good girl, Lola but make sure you get it all," encouraged Miranda as she raised the paddle above her head. "Now you could learn something from my maid, Jean for she knows how to behave, at least some of the time.!

"Yes, Mistress," winced Jean as the first loud slap exploded over his buttocks.

He was always shocked at his mistress' strength when she was laying into him with her instruments of correction but the paddle was one of her favourites. She loved the resounding sound of the wide leather blade as it impacted on the soft flesh of her victims.

Jean jumped in agony each time she brought the paddle down on his glowing checks but he meekly accepted the punishment that his confined passion had earned him. This was his lot as the slave cabin boy of the pirate Miranda so he had no other option but to simply endure.

Once Lola had licked up all the salty tasting come from the box she pulled herself up so that she could tell her mistress. She watched Miranda spank Jean a couple more times before she announced that she had completed her task, after all it was all his fault that she had been dragged from her slumbers in the first place.

"Well done, Lola: now you can help me to get dressed whilst Jean gets my breakfast.," said Miranda approvingly. "And no pants for you, my lad - only your short apron so everyone can see how naughty you have been."

Jean scampered away from the cabin again with only a small piece of cloth covering his loins and his scarlet buttocks bare for all to see. He knew that the men would see what Miranda had done to him which would make them laugh heartily once more at his expense.

As Jean squirmed in the galley waiting for Miranda's food Lola helped her mistress to bathe with precious drinking water. She sponged down every inch of Miranda's body until her mistress was clean but also in a minor frenzy of excitement after having such loving attention lavished on her.

Spanking Jean had really turned Miranda on but Lola had sent her over the edge so she demanded that the young maid lick her pussy instantly. As she got out of the tin bath she spread her legs so that Lola could fall to her knees with her face at the correct height for serving her mistress. Needing no second invitation Lola buried her head in Miranda's short pubic mound her eager tongue delving between her mistress' moist labia. The delicious taste of Miranda's juices soon began to mingle with the tang of Jean's semen until Lola's head spun in delight.

Lola loved to serve which was just as well for she had served between her mistress' legs ever since she had been purchased at a slave auction on the tiny pirate island of St. Gido many

116

months before. With the exception of a privileged few of Miranda's guests she had only served her mistress although she had been made to suck Jean's cock several times for Miranda's amusement when he had been a good boy. She liked the taste of the good looking French boy but she preferred it when she was ordered to licked his semen out of her mistress' pussy, which was a very rare treat.

Happily Lola lapped away at Miranda's oozing sex forcing her velvet tongue up between her quivering lips. She caressed the sodden wall of Miranda's vagina until her mistress was gyrating with pleasure above her obviously ready to come.

With one last thrust into Miranda's pussy Lola ensured that her mistress enjoyed the full force of an immensely satisfying orgasm. This left mistress and maid happy at the start of their day for Lola knew that she would not be punished, at least not yet.

Miranda was also pleased to start her day in this sensuous way, finally being able to relax to the extent that she could concentrate on what she must do to hold her men. As Lola licked her juices away she had an idea that she was sure would convince all her men to continue to follow her over the Seven Seas.

Once Lola had helped her squeeze into her tight pants as well as the rest of her revealing outfit Miranda ate the breakfast that the highly embarrassed Jean presented to her on his knees. The cook had teased him about his nakedness and his red buttocks so he was desperate to get back into her good books.

Instead Miranda made him get down on all fours whilst she ate off his bare back before leaving him there as she went off to address her men. He would have to stay in that exact position until Miranda deigned to return to use him no doubt as furniture once again.

117

If fact Miranda had no immediate plans to return for she was on a mission that she wanted to share with her assembled men. She remembered that the Governor of Hispaniola was due to return to Spain in a couple of days so she informed her crew that they would be going after his ship The Santa Brava.

At first the men would have nothing of it for The Santa Brava was a much stronger ship than Miranda's Revenge. But Miranda eventually persuaded them to go along with her when she told them what would actually be on the Spanish ship.

She explained to them that The Santa Brava would have most of the gold and silver taken from Central America that winter. It would also be carrying the ladies of the Governor's Court who would be returning to Spain for the summer including the Governor's charming daughter the Contessa de Marono.

Miranda had a special reason for wanting to meet the Contessa again but she did not want to share that with the crew even if they ever captured The Santa Brava.

"If we are lucky, the Governor himself might even be aboard then we'll have some fun with him," shouted Miranda to her excited audience. "When we've finished with him we'll see what we can get for him at the slave market."

"Not a lot, I wager, the great oaf," replied Williams, her second in command as well as her occasional lover.

Miranda was pleased that he seamed to like her plan for although it was dangerous the rewards were clearly fantastic. They would risk a lot but Miranda would give anything to have the Contessa at her mercy after what she had done.

With a whoop of joy the crew set to the task of turning Miranda's Revenge towards her intended target in the west. With the wind set fair they would sight Hispaniola in less than a day and be in position to attack The Santa Brava once it cleared the port guns on the shore.

The crew worked hard with the sails and the wind all day so that Miranda's Revenge was in a great position by the evening to greet the emergence of The Santa Brava with the pre-dawn tide. Miranda was so pleased with her men that she gave them the rest of the night off which meant all kinds of hell for the two poor sluts in the hold. But Miranda didn't care about that as she returned to her cabin for she was on the verge of gaining the revenge for which she had named her ship after all those years ago. As she opened the door of her room all he could think about was what she was going to do with the Contessa in the morning when they took The Santa Brava.

It wasn't until she saw Jean still kneeling on the floor that she realised that she had left him there all day

"Oh, my poor baby, have you been like that all day?" asked Miranda, her voice dangerously sweet.

"Yes, Mistress," replied an exhausted Jean.

"Well you have been a very good boy and I think it is time for you to be rewarded," she breathed seductively.

Thoughts of the Contessa at her mercy had softened Miranda to the point that she was prepared to let Jean have his wicked way with her. She ordered her slave boy to crawl over to her bed where she was already shedding the skin of her clothes.

"Lie on the bed, you little angel and I will show you the best time of your short life," said Miranda as she dropped the last of her clothes to the floor.

1Jean scampered over to her bed his cock already stiffening between his legs at the promise made by his mistress. He clambered onto the bed with the excitement of a child let loose on its first Christmas toy.

"Now put your arms over your head, young man, for we must still keep you under control," ordered Miranda as she produced a length of rope from her cupboard.

"Yes, Mistress," he replied instantly flinging his hands to either edge of the small bed head above him.

Miranda quickly tied Jean's wrists to the bed before climbing on top of his squirming body with her thighs straddling his hips. She felt his hard penis rubbing against her moist labia as he tried to get into a better position below her.

"Steady on, tiger; let's see what you can do with these first!" chided Miranda as she shoved her breasts into the boy's face.

Jeans eagerly licked Miranda's erect nipples but he desperately wanted to plunge his member up into her pussy that was so tantalisingly close yet so far away. If he made his move too early his mistress would have him flayed alive so he had to wait his turn.

So he lay as still as he could whilst his mistress tormented him with her beautiful body whilst he squirmed beneath her. He licked her candy pink nipples with all the fervour of a slave boy trying to get into his mistress' good books once more.

"Now there's a good boy and not so little any more," breathed Miranda starting to rub her swollen clitoris against Jean's stiff manhood.

1She loved it when Jean licked her nipples especially as he was trying to impress her so that she would let him screw her. Little did the poor boy know that she was equally desperate to get his cock inside her but she wanted to make him work hard before she allowed them both the ultimate pleasure.

As her nipples tingled with the pleasure that Jean was arousing in them Miranda knew it was high time that she put them both out of their misery. She carefully lifted herself up before lowering herself in ecstasy onto Jean's bursting penis.

"Ooh, I'd almost forgotten what a big boy you are," sighed Miranda as Jean's cock filled her gaping hole. "After all it has been so long since I allowed you to do this to me."

"Yes, Mistress, thank you Mistress," moaned Jean as all his

dreams came true

Miranda began to ride her slave boy as his penis slipped in and out of her well-lubricated pussy each stroke making her shiver with delight. She could feel a massive surge of energy building up inside her, which she could hold off no longer for she knew that she simply had to surrender to her inevitable orgasm.

With a scream of pure happiness Miranda came with an intensity made more acute by the fact that she had resisted the temptation to jump straight on Jean's straining member. Because she had made herself wait the blast of ecstasy that shot through her very being was much stronger as well as more satisfying than if she had immediately succumbed to her carnal desires.

As she passed the peak of her excitement she pinched Jean's nipples as hard as she could, which in turn triggered his own orgasm. He cried out as he came for he knew that he was forbidden from shooting his seed into his mistress but he had been given no choice by the position that he was in.

"Have you come inside me, you naughty little boy?" demanded Miranda menacingly.

"I am sorry, Mistress but it was when you nipped me...I just couldn't control myself."

"Well, who's going to clean this up?" Miranda inquired pointing to the sperm dripping from her sex as she climbed off Jean's still hard cock.

"We could get Lola to do it, I know you like to watch her work," suggested Jean hoping that she wouldn't make him do it.

"You lazy dog, you prefer to get a woman to clear up your disgusting mess," said Miranda with a dangerous look in her eyes.

"Yes, Mistress, sorry Mistress..." said Jean pathetically.

Miranda wandered over to the door in order to scream down the passageway for her maid to come and assist her. Lola knew what to do even if this scum did not although Miranda would certainly make him pay dearly for his lack of self-control.

"Yes, Mistress, you called me," said Lola entering the room.

"Get on your knees and lick this slime out of me whilst I think of what to do with this sea dog over there," ordered Maria.

"Yes, Mistress," replied Lola dropping to her knees instantly before Miranda's spread legs.

She could see Jean's sperm dribbling down the inside of her mistress' thighs so she began to lap it up with her long tongue. Again the salty tang of Jean's issue accosted her taste buds making her want to swallow every precious drop as well as wish that Jean had been allowed to cum deep inside her pussy instead of Miranda's.

"There's a good girl," said Miranda her again leaving her with every stroke of the girl's velvet tongue. "Now what shall I do with him?"

Once Lola had cleaned her mistress' pussy Miranda decided that Jean could go back in the box for the duration of the fight. She would release him later once the Contessa was safely on board and at her mercy. He might be able to help her extract her own special brand of revenge on the slut.

Following Miranda's instructions Lola released Jean from the bed before tying his hands behind his back at wrist as well as at elbows. Once he was secure she helped Jean to climb into the box that she locked shut with her mistress' heavy padlock.

Her next task was to assist her mistress get ready for the coming battle by helping her to get dressed. Miranda decided that she would put one of her finest dresses on to meet the Contessa because she had faith in her men's ability to do all the fighting for her.

"Very good, Lola," Miranda said, looking at her reflection

in her beautiful light blue silk dress. "Now we will go and catch the morning's quarry together."

Lola followed Miranda out to the quarterdeck from where she could command the coming battle. Her men were all ready with the weapons and as if right on cue Miranda could see The Santa Brava gliding through the water towards them.

"Ok boys, I want the Governor and the Contessa alive but you can do what you want with the rest, especially the women," cried Miranda. "Now open fire and get the bastards!"

In an instant all hell broke loose as the crew of Miranda's Revenge fired several broadsides at The Santa Brava then moved alongside the Spanish galleon in order to board her. In a blaze of colour Miranda's men stormed across onto the smoke filled decks of the already stricken ship. Miranda watched with pride as her crew easily overcame the Spanish Marines who tumbled half clothed onto the deck to fight. In less than half an hour it was all over and The Santa Brava had been taken by Miranda's pirates.

She ordered the skeleton crew on board The Santa Brava to follow Miranda's Revenge at a safe distance until they were well away from the attentions of the shore batteries. For the moment the Spanish survivors were stowed below on their former ship whilst Miranda's crew grappled with the ship's acres of sail.

Eventually she decided that they were far enough away to carry out a transfer of her prey to Miranda's Revenge before they continued their journey to even safer waters. A longboat was launched and immediately pulled for The Santa Brava to retrieve what for Miranda was its most valuable cargo.

Miranda could not take her eyes off the little boat as its precious goods were loaded aboard before setting out on its homeward journey. Miranda just could make out the Governor in his nightshirt shivering in the morning air alongside his pretty daughter the Contessa.

Miranda's nipples were rock hard once again as the tiny boat pulled up beside Revenge for she could hardly contain her excitement. The name of Miranda's ship now became completely appropriate for at last these two dogs who had made her suffer so much were finally at her mercy.

"Ah, good morning your Excellency, so sorry to wake you so early," said Miranda sarcastically to her guests as they were manhandled aboard Revenge.

"Who the hell are you?" demanded the Governor desperately trying to regain the upper hand.

"Why, don't you remember me?" asked Miranda sweetly. "I'm the English girl you captured, used and abused then sold into slavery."

"It's Miranda, Father," said the Contessa her voice quaking with fear.

"That's right and I have waited for this moment for far too long," said Miranda with a dangerous glint in her eye.

She eyed the young Contessa with her flowing raven black hair and her petite figure clad only in her white satin nightdress. She was scared stiff but still haughty and devastatingly pretty just as she had been all those nights that she had tortured poor Miranda in her father's dungeons.

"So what are you going to do with us?" whispered the Governor humbled by the realisation that he had fallen into the hands of one of his former victims.

"Well first I am going to flog you and your lovely daughter as you flogged me and then I am going to torture the pair of you for a couple of days," responded Miranda as if she was reading her choice from a menu.

"And what will happen to us after that?" asked the Contessa, her lips beginning to tremble as her fear over came her.

"I will sell you on the same island where you sold me, and

your father will be ransomed to the King of Spain himself," replied Miranda triumphantly.

"But you can't, I'm the Governor of..."

"I know exactly who you are," interrupted Miranda. "I should know for I spent long enough enjoying your hospitality!"

"But we can pay you..." spluttered the Contessa.

"Yes you can pay and you will pay, believe me, for every second I was at your mercy and it starts right now," said Miranda and turning to her men she shouted. "Take this bitch to my quarters and string the Governor up with the rest of the meat."

Miranda watched some of her men take the Governor away towards the stores before following the men who were dragging the Contessa to her fate. She struggled as the men pulled her along but she stood no chance against the brawny sailors who dealt with her as easily as a child especially once they had bound her hands behind her back.

Miranda loved the way the girl's nipples were already straining against the flimsy material of her nightdress even though she was in such grave danger. She was going to enjoy her revenge immensely and then make a tidy profit on this slut who had tormented her endlessly.

Before she followed her prey into her cabin she told the men that everything else and everybody else on The Santa Brava was theirs to do with as they wanted. The cheers resulting from this generous offer were still ringing in her ears as she closed the door behind her.

"Well, my dear it hasn't been a good day for you so far and it is only going to get worse, I can assure you," crowed Miranda.

"Leave me alone, you can't treat me like this!" cried the Contessa sounding as brave as she possibly could under the circumstances.

"I don't think that you are in a position to tell me what to do any more, young lady," said Miranda imperiously. "In fact I would say that the boot is definitely on the other foot now."

As if to emphasise her total dominance of the situation she released Jean from his box so that he could help her with her plans for her captive. Jean climbed wearily out of his tiny wooden prison before dropping to his knees at his mistress' feet in abject gratitude at being released.

"Now Jean you can help me string this little bitch up so we can show her who is boss around here," said Miranda in a deceptively friendly voice untying the boy's bonds.

In a trice Jean undid the Contessa's wrists while she simply stood watching him, his naked body making her too stunned to react. She had never seen a man in this state before because she had led a very sheltered life. Her father had not even allowed her to have any suitors let alone see them naked so she could hardly take her eyes off this boy's glistening body.

As she stared at the boy he began to rip the flimsy satin nightdress from her shaking shoulders leaving her as naked as he was before her new mistress. The poor Contessa could then only watch as this character that had just crawled out of his box before her began to bind her into an even more compromising position.

On Miranda's instructions Jean bound the Contessa's wrists tightly together in front of her with a long length of ship's rope before making her stand on a low stool in the centre of the room. He then proceeded to throw the loose end of the rope over one of the beams holding up the ceiling of Miranda's cabin.

Once he had secured the rope to the beam with the Contessa's arms stretched above her he pulled the buffet away. This left her dangling several inches above the floor with all the weight of her voluptuous body hanging on her dainty wrists.

"Ow, that hurts so much, Miranda," squealed the Contessa.

126

"Let me down at once, I order you!"

"Now, now, my dear, you are no longer in a position to order me around," chided Miranda as she walked towards her suspended prey. "In fact I am about to demonstrate just how much the tables have turned for you, with my lovely little whip."

For the first time the Contessa noticed that Miranda was fondling a wicked looking black leather whip in her hands with long lashes flowing from its tightly braided handle. She shuddered with fear as she hung from the beam wondering exactly how much pain she was going to inflict.

For her part Miranda knew precisely what she was going to do with her but she decided to size up her victim first. Strolling round the girl strung up before her like a side of meat Miranda was pleased to note that the Contessa was just as attractive as the day she had breezed into Miranda's cell all those years ago.

"My, my, I am going to get a good price for you at auction," said Miranda admiring the Contessa's firm breasts and long coltish legs.

"You will never sell me because my father..."

"Is currently hanging in the larder waiting for his punishment and therefore cannot do anything to help you this time," interrupted Miranda. "In fact I might let Lola loose on him with a bull whip to add to his humiliation."

"You can't do that," spluttered the Contessa concerned for her father's welfare despite her own obvious predicament.

"I can and I will," Miranda insisted. "In fact, to make it more interesting I might make you watch then join in!"

"That's horrible, you simply mustn't..."

"Oh but I must for you did far worse to me in your father's dungeon," said Miranda. "And you enjoyed every minute of it."

"But I was..."

127

"Only obeying orders, I know but you had a whale of a time making me suffer so now it's my turn," snapped Miranda then truing to Jean she said, "Now silence this bitch whilst I roast her hide for her!"

Jean proceed to stuff a wad of old cloth into the squirming Contessa's mouth that he secured in place with a short wide belt. This slotted between her teeth before being fastened at the back of her slender neck.

Thereafter the Contessa could make nothing more than a muffled squawk through her gag even when Miranda slashed at her buttocks viciously with her whip. What pathetic sounds she could make were instantly drowned by the loud crack as the merciless lashes impacted upon her defenceless body.

So determined was Miranda to extract revenge on the Contessa that she flogged her as hard as she could for half an hour hardly pausing for breath. Consequently she was panting hard when she finally took a step back in order to examine her handiwork.

The Contessa's body was a mass of angry red weals with seemingly every inch of her tender flesh covered with the marks left by the relentless whip. The poor girl hung in constant pain but Miranda had no sympathy for her whatsoever.

She remembered vividly the times the Contessa had her in a similar position in a dark damp cell with her feet vainly searching for the support of the cold stone floor. The Contessa had had no mercy on her on many similar occasions instead preferring to flog Miranda raw before leaving her to hang in misery for the rest of the night.

"So, now you know how it feels, you bitch, to be strung up and beaten without pity," snarled Miranda.

"Please let me go, I beg of you..." moaned the Contessa once Miranda had loosened her gag so that she could reply.

"No way, madam, because we're only just getting started,"

insisted Miranda.

"No, please, I can't take any more..."

"I seem to remember saying that myself as you flogged me under your palace, but you ignored my pleas for mercy and therefore so shall I," said Miranda shoving the Contessa's gag back in place to stifle any further entreaties from her.

As Miranda prepared to whip the Contessa again she could feel her own nipples straining against the material of her dress. The tiny dribble of liquid down her inner thighs also told her that her pussy was wet with all the excitement of punishing her.

Miranda had not bothered to put on any undergarments in her haste to get hold of the Contessa so her thighs were soon coated with her own moistness. This, she decided, needed to be cleaned off so she ordered Jean to crawl under her skirts whilst she spread her legs.

Jean knew exactly what to do once he was on his knees between his mistress' firm thighs so as Miranda raised the whip above her head again he stuck out his tongue. In the stuffy darkness under Miranda's skirts Jean was able to locate his mistress' pussy by the strong odour of arousal above him.

Once he had found Miranda's sodden labia he began to lick between the well-lubricated lips in his pitch-black search for her clitoris. His quest was not in vain for he soon felt her swollen bud with the end of his tongue so he began to lap away at his mistress' most sensitive flesh.

In between the shuddering of the hard strokes that Miranda was dealing out to the Contessa above him he could feel his mistress' sex quivering as his lips closed around it. As he became bolder he started to nibble Miranda's engorged clit gently with his teeth.

This was a dangerous game for if he hurt Miranda he would be in serious trouble but if he got it just right she would have a rapturous orgasm. One result could lead to a great reward whereas the other would most certainly lead to the sort of treatment being meted out to the poor Contessa.

Luckily for Jean he managed to get it just right for after a few minutes of the lavish attention that he was paying to Miranda's clit his mistress came. Jean could feel the shivers vibrating deep within Miranda's sex as her orgasm flowed through her entire trembling body.

Miranda's ecstatic reaction to Jean's efforts on her behalf were so intense that she dropped her whip thus giving the relieved Contessa a break from her painful onslaught. As she simply hung there enveloped in agony she could only watch her captor enjoying the throes of rapture.

When she had recovered from her excitement Miranda ensured that Jean cleaned off all her juices with his expert tongue by grabbing his hair through her dress. She pulled his head up between her legs until she was sure that he'd adequately cleaned her.

"Very good Jean, you have learned well all that I taught you," she said pulling aside her skirts to allow him to get back on his feet. "Now it's time for the Contessa's pussy to get some attention but not in quite the same way."

Miranda directed Jean to cut her victim down who promptly fell to the floor in an agonised heap panting with relief. The Contessa's release was short lived however because Jean immediately forced her onto her back before tying each of her wrists to each ankle with the discarded pieces of rope.

The Contessa was soon helpless once again but to make matters worse Jean knelt over her straddling her face whilst at the same time pulling her bound arms and legs back. Because he held the Contessa's thighs under his armpits her sex was cruelly exposed below him, an open invitation for use or abuse.

"So, Jean, you played that game with my pussy and now it

130

is my turn to play it with your balls," said Miranda mischievously.

"Yes, Mistress?" replied Jean nervously.

"Well, boy, just as you thought you could risk bringing me pain in a trade off for pleasure then so will I, first with your balls then your lovely cock," explained Miranda. "You will place your balls in this slut's mouth whilst I whip her slit here."

"But what if she..."

"She won't , will you my dear, unless I hit her really hard," said Miranda not entirely reassuringly. "But if it helps I will threaten to hang her by her thumbs before flogging her breasts if she bites you."

"Thank you, Mistress, " said Jean his thoughts now plagued with images of the Contessa biting off his precarious balls.

"Now, Contessa, open up and take young Jean's balls into your pretty little mouth," ordered Miranda once she had pulled the gag from her mouth again.

Jean felt a furious shaking of the maiden's head below his manhood but Miranda, seeing the Contessa's disobedience simply grabbed one of her beauty lips between her strong fingers.

"Open up I said, or else I'll pinch this as hard as I can," threatened Miranda.

The Contessa, already moaning in pain through gritted teeth opened her mouth to allow Jean to gingerly to insert his trembling testicles. She had heard what Miranda had said about the dire punishment for biting Jean so she cradled his balls within her lips as carefully as she could.

She immediately tasted the salty residue of Jean's earlier encounter with his mistress but this was enhanced by the aroma of Jean's hot body. Between Jean's legs the Contessa could see Jean's anus which she thought would revolt her but which fascinated her intensely.

She had never been exposed to such treatment so she knew

that she should have been disgusted but in reality she enjoyed the thought of being under this boy. She found herself unbelievably wanting to actually lick between Jean's taut buttocks even as he actually sat down on her face to relieve the pressure on his balls.

"There's a good girl, you're learning," said Miranda patronisingly. "Now, Jean, grab her beauty lips and pull them apart as far as you can."

"Yes, Mistress," sighed Jean enjoying every second of having his balls immersed in the warm wetness of the Contessa's mouth.

As Jean pulled apart the Contessa's labia Miranda could see the bud of her clitoris emerging from the stretched folds of skin. She smiled broadly for it was swollen and glistening with the first dew of the Contessa's arousal.

"So, you randy little bitch, you are enjoying yourself, aren't you?" she demanded nastily.

The Contessa shook her head as vigorously as she could under the circumstances but Miranda already knew the answer to her question.

"Well, if that is the case then we are going to have to do something about it," continued Miranda wandering off to select a switch made of slender bamboo.

She had cut this herself from a tree on one of the islands knowing full well that it would someday bring exquisite pain to someone, and that day had come. With a glint of real pleasure in her eyes she raised the cane high above her head before slashing it down between her victim's cruelly separated thighs.

The Contessa screamed loudly into her fleshy gag for the thin rod caught her exactly across her hardened clit. She was desperate to clench her teeth in agony but she knew that this would lead inevitably to even more pain for her.

Once again the cane whistled its terrifying song as it sped

towards its quivering target. Another deafening crack followed by the Contessa's muffled screaming revealed the fact that the cane had once more found its mark.

The agony that the previous beating had inflicted upon her helpless body was now eclipsed by this fresh wave of pain emanating from her tenderised vulva. Each time Miranda's evil switch found its fragile mark the Contessa continued to scream pitifully not daring to bite down in anguish however much she wanted to.

Miranda on the other hand was thoroughly enjoying herself for she remembered with every stroke the tortures that the Contessa had inflicted on her.

But was a long way to St. Gido and it would not do to wear the bitch out on the first morning so she decided that her captive had received enough punishment for the moment.

"Alright, Jean, that's enough for the moment," announced Miranda. "Now shove your cock in her mouth and give her something to taste!"

"Yes, Mistress," said Jean joyfully as he carefully shifted position.

He withdrew his balls from the Contessa's mouth with a loud plop before replacing it with his stiffened ramrod. He smiled to himself as he heard the haughty looking Contessa gagging on his cock but he simply plunged it deeper into her mouth.

After a few hard jerks Jean felt himself coming so with one last push he emptied himself in the Contessa's throat. Groaning with immense satisfaction Jean leaned forward to plant a kiss between the Contessa's labia which he had inadvertently pulled even further apart when he came.

"Ah, how touching, he gives her a thank-you kiss," said Miranda sarcastically. "Now get her into the box because I want to go and have some fun with the Governor."

Jean extracted himself from his position on the floor with the Contessa then lifted her easily in his arms. Miranda had already opened the box so Jean just dumped the Contessa in it prior to locking the lid shut above her crumpled form.

Once Miranda was sure that the chest was secure she covered her exquisite body with her robe and led her slave-boy still naked up onto the deck to see what her men were up to. What she saw was like Dante's Inferno with all manner of debasement going on all over the ship.

The poor ladies of the Spanish Colonial Court were being ravished all around her in various types of bondage. Miranda felt another shiver of excitement ripple through her as she watched a large pirate ramming his penis into the anus of a woman who was bound over one of the guns with her legs spread obscenely wide.

Another woman had been strung upside down after being stripped and was being used by a gang of men who were taking it in turns to rape her mouth with their straining cocks. Another larger woman was being flogged mercilessly by two men who stood in front and behind her as she hung limply by thick ropes from a boom.

Miranda laughed out loud for she was sorely tempted to join in the fun but she had bigger fish to fry so she headed off to the store room with her faithful servant in tow.

When she found the Governor he was trussed up naked in a hog-tie like a chicken in the storeroom with his arms bound behind him with thin wire. His legs were curled back up his back but the most devilish part was that he had been suspended above the floor by a rope running from his joined ankles and wrists to the ceiling.

"Not so regal now are you, you scumbucket?" said Miranda nastily as she prodded the writhing man in the ribs with the handle of her bullwhip.

The Governor could not reply as Miranda's men had bound a pair of Lola's undergarments into his mouth with rope. Instead he grunted loudly especially when Miranda grabbed his cock which hung uselessly below him.

Because the Governor's lifestyle had enabled him to become a portly fellow over the years Miranda decided that she could not be bothered torturing him. Instead she tied a thin piece of wire with a hook on the end of it around the base of his scrotum.

She then took a large cheese from one of the larder shelves which she attached to the wire thus putting even more pressure on the Governor's stretched balls. Another cheese increased the tension further, making Miranda's victim moan into his gag for release.

"I think that Lola would enjoy torturing this bastard so cut along and get her Jean," said Miranda kicking the cheeses to make them swing.

"Yes, Mistress," giggled Jean running off to bring the maid back.

"You see, Mr. Governor, I give poor Lola a hard time and she likes to get her own back occasionally," explained Miranda. "I can see that she will have great fun with you!"

The Governor merely grunted as Jean scampered back with an excited Lola in tow. She had been watching the men as they dealt with their new captives but when Jean explained that her mistress was going to let her play with one herself she could hardly contain herself.

"Ah, Lola, I want you to meet the Governor of Hispaniola who is our guest," said Miranda handing the girl her coiled bullwhip. "I want you to make him feel even more uncomfortable if you can, and remember that this bastard tortured me on his rack for days without mercy!"

"Yes, Mistress," replied Lola.

It was true that Miranda made Lola's life a misery on occasion but usually only when she had been a naughty girl. In fact she loved her mistress so the thought of this man torturing her made Lola so mad that she was determined to make him suffer.

"So, you bilge rat, you hurt my mistress did you?" snarled Lola as she yanked his head back by his hair. "Well you may think that you're in pain now but wait 'til I've finished with you..."

"That's a good girl," laughed Miranda as she led Jean from the storeroom back towards her room. "Everything seems to be in order, don't you think?"

"Oh yes, Mistress," replied the fawning Jean.

"So it's time we paid that little madam another visit," continued Miranda. "And helped her on her journey into servitude."

"Yes, Mistress," said Jean following her like a faithful puppy.

The object of Miranda's attention was trying to recover from her ordeal, although still being imprisoned in the chest with her wrists bound to her ankles it was almost impossible. She tried to spit Jean's come out of her mouth but he had planted it so deep in her throat that she couldn't get rid of the distinctive taste.

It wasn't that she found it abhorrent or that she even objected to having his large penis thrust into her mouth. She would simply have preferred to get to know Jean on her terms instead of being tied up and at the tender mercy of a woman that she had formerly had the pleasure of torturing herself.

It was scary to think that now she was the captive with no chance of escape however it was also undeniably exciting. Her pussy still ached from the beating she had received but even in the cramped box the Contessa could not resist trying to reach round to finger her swollen moist lips.

Eventually, and with much difficulty she managed to slide her fingers between her labia and into the entrance of her sodden vagina. She shivered at the delicious pain of scraping the walls of her pussy with her long nails which was intensified every time she brushed against her throbbing clit with her knuckles.

Perhaps, she felt, there was something to receiving pain as well as giving it. Even though she had made herself wet with arousal every time she had flogged prisoners such as Miranda in her father's dungeons she had wondered all along how it would feel to be captured.

The idea of being treated like a base slave had tortured her nights for years now but she had never summoned up the courage to explore her fantasies. Now they had been forced upon her so she could expunge the guilt of all those thoughts of serving a master or mistress in chains and live the fantasy instead.

Her fingers dashed in and out of her sex as she relived the beatings that her new mistress had already given her. She had always felt awkward about playing with herself for fear of being caught but now it was marvellous to be able to masturbate freely, despite the close confines of the box.

Just as Miranda burst into her room to see her prey the Contessa came with a violent scream that shocked even her new owner. Miranda stood in the doorway to listen to the long protracted sobs coming from the old chest realising immediately that these were cries of joy not anguish.

"Well, Jean, it seems that tied up in the darkness of your box the Contessa has found her true place in society," mused Miranda staring at the now quiet box. "And, if that is the case, I might just keep the little slut for myself after all."

"Yes, Mistress," sighed Jean contentedly.

I did not believe that our army had actually won until I saw our men parade triumphantly through the streets of the capital Sarmizegethusa with their Roman prisoners following behind.

In direct contrast to the proud Dacian soldiers with their shields and spears the Romans were stark naked wearing only the chains of their captors. They were being led past cheering crowds for the most part by young pretty girls whose pride shone through as they dragged their captives along, faces cast down in total defeat.

Our leader, the great Burebista had decreed that all those who had been widowed by the Emperor Trajan and his Roman legions had earned the right to greet the victorious Dacian troops. He had then said that these women could try to appease the pain of their losses by dragging their tormentors through the streets then torturing them or keeping them as slaves.

I had not bothered to participate, even though my husband Xavier had been killed by Roman scouts on the banks of the Danube several years before. I had grieved a long time so I stayed away to avoid reopening old wounds. But I did go to look down on those strong muscular men from that distant warlike land following our women as humbly as dogs, reduced to nothing without their swords and armour. I even noticed that some woman were leading two or three men each so I went out to speak with then as they walked by my house.

"So Burebista was telling the truth was he?" I asked a buxom woman who had a couple of young dark haired boys in tow.

"Well you can see from this lot that Burebista has not let us down," replied the woman almost breathless with excitement of pulling her prizes with her.

"Where are you taking them?" I enquired, intrigued as to

the fate of these beaten men struggling in their bonds before me.

"To the main square then to my villa where I intend to string them up then thrash them both with my late husband's dog whip," she said simply.

"But why do you want to do this to them?" I enquired somewhat naively.

"Because their comrades killed my husband by the Danube and now I am going to make them pay," she answered.

"But that's where my man was killed," I responded in a daze.

"Get yourself one or two of these then and remind yourself that your man did not die in vain," urged the woman.

With a tug on the chains she continued her journey down the street towards her home where her two prisoners were in for a torrid time. The woman had a shapely body and swung her hips as she walked away from me but I was sure that she would swing her husband's whip with even more enthusiasm.

Despite my earlier reservations I was fascinated at the prospect of having one of these prized specimens in my power. I went off to talk to a nearby Dacian guard. He told me that all I had to do was prove to his captain that I was a war widow then I could take any man or men I chose.

Fully wrapped up in the emotion of the event I ran up to the captain to explain my eligibility. He told me that there were even more men coming at the back of the column who had not been claimed by any of the widows.

I thanked him but wondered what dregs of society had been ignored by the haughty women who were still strutting past me. All thoughts of my poor husband were gone as I watched ranks of lowly hostages file past me with their mouths cruelly gagged with heavy wooden bits.

With nothing but Dacian chains to hide their rippling muscular I found myself wishing to my shame that I would end up with one as good looking as these fallen Roman gods. I did not hold out much hope though for no Dacian woman in her right mind would allow any of these boys to go unclaimed.

I watched with envy every woman who passed by with her man bound in disgrace behind her knowing that I would not be lucky. I wanted a piece of this action because for the first time since my husband had marched off to war I was beginning to feel aroused at the thought of male flesh.

Eventually the women began to thin out but the flow of captured Romans did not so I decided to grasp my opportunity as it came up. The rest of the Romans were guarded by ordinary soldiers so I told one of them what the captain had said. He told me to pick out one or two for myself then join the parade with the rest of the women.

It was not an easy task picking a couple of men from so many fine examples of manliness but I did not have much time. The column was still moving so I picked out two tall prisoners with jet-black hair and handsome faces hidden behind their painful gags.

"Alright Miss, just take the chains from the guards holding them," said the soldier. "Then join the other women with their slaves to show that you own them."

"Thank you sir," I said dragging my acquisitions away with me towards the other new slave owners.

I had never owned slaves before although it was common for Dacian families to have at least two around the house. Some people even had sex slaves captured from the Greek port towns along the Black Sea coast but I had never even considered the prospect of owning another human being.

The victory parade however had changed my mind for I now saw a way to avenge my husband's death as well as bring some happiness back into my life. So I led my slave boys past

140

the cheering crowds as proudly as the other widows thinking all the while what I would do with the pair of them.

Looking at the cheering people lining our route I thought how wonderful it was to taste victory after all the defeats at the hands of the Romans. Now it was my turn along with all the other widows to get our own back for years of torment at their hands.

I decided that I would follow the buxom lady's advice for giving these slave boys a good flogging which would at least clear my system of anger. My friend Aridar could help me to deal with them for even though she had never lost anybody in the war she wouldn't want to pass up the opportunity to get even with them.

By the time the parade reached the main square I was thoroughly aroused at the thought of whipping my slave boys. I couldn't wait to scourge these heartless invaders of our land, then perhaps I would investigate the other possibilities that having two naked slave boys to hand would throw up.

But before I went I wanted to see what the authorities were going to do with the other captives in the square before I rushed off home with mine.

The centre of the city was full of cheering crowds but what caught my attention was the large platform erected in front of the temple. It was raised several feet above the ground so that more people could see what was going to happen up there. I noticed that there were four unusual devices set at each corner of the dais like fence posts about four feet high. I could not understand their purpose at first for they were made of a very strange wooden design culminating in a phallic shape at the top.

Each one had another piece of wood across it three feet long about a foot off the floor with leather straps dangling from the ends. Protruding from the upright pole on a short metal bar six inches from the top was a small horseshoe which had me totally bemused until I saw what they were going to be used for.

One of the generals of Burebista's army climbed onto the platform in order to address the over-animated crowd.

"People of Dacia I offer you these leaders of the Roman army as a symbol of our great victory over their comrades," he cried to loud cheers. "They will remain here during the auctioning of their troops then for the rest of the week for you to jeer at and deride!"

The cheering became deafening as four Roman soldiers were dragged up onto the platform by some of the general's men. They were already naked like the rest of the captives but their torsos were covered in the deep red marks of the floggings they had already received from some of the Dacian widows.

The Romans had had their wrists chained up their backs to thick metal collars locked around their necks. This meant that they were already uncomfortable but this was nothing compared with what happened to them once they reached their allotted posts.

The Dacian soldiers lifted each man up then rammed them down onto the phallus like tips of the poles. I winced as I realised that the end of the poles must have entered the Roman soldiers' anuses which must have hurt terribly.

The Dacian troops then spread their enemies' legs before securing their ankles with the straps to the ends of the cross poles. This meant that the majority of the weight of these poor wretches rested upon the phalluses deep within them, alleviated only slightly by their being able to touch their toes to the crossbars.

The reason for the horseshoes also became clear as the Dacians callously flipped the genitals of their victims over the upturned 'u' shapes. This pulled them forward presumably for better public display as well as even more pain for the helplessly tortured souls.

Once the Dacian soldiers had finished their task they left the four former leaders of the Roman elite guard to suffer like contorted ships' figureheads in constant torment. I could see that it was only the brutal wooden gags stuffed into their mouths which prevented them from screaming out in agony.

The Dacian soldiers were replaced by six priestesses from the temple who were going to oversee the sale of the rest of the captured Roman troops. They were resplendent in their brief shifts of purest white which fell to their thighs barely hiding their voluptuous figures.

In their hands I saw that they carried long leather chariot whips with which they were going to keep order amongst the slaves. I could not help but admire the graceful way they conducted themselves even as the first men were shoved up the steps to the auction block.

The crowds surged forward to see the goods on display wondering how much the slaves would fetch once the bidding started. The money was going to widows and orphans from the war but people would still want the cheapest male flesh that they could lay their hands on.

From the very first young man to be presented to the excited punters the bidding was fast and furious with very high prices being offered for the fittest or most handsome slaves. Men came then went from the platform in a continuous flow rattling chains before being whisked off to various parts of the city by their new owners.

In a sense these were the lucky ones because the men who had been chosen by the widows gathered that morning at the edge of the city were in for a pretty torrid time. I had already seen one woman lashing out at her slave-boy with a stick in a towering rage for dawdling too far behind her.

For my part I only felt sadness at the loss of my husband for we were still young and childless although I understood the anger experienced by some of the women who had lost loved ones. I did wonder whether having these two slave boys to beat at my leisure would help take the away pain that I still felt.

I watched the lovely priestesses a little while longer before turning for home pulling my slaves behind me. How could I have been so greedy as to demand two of these specimens? I began to wonder what on earth I was going to do with them.

As I walked along I reasoned that I could always sell one of them to help pay for the upkeep of the villa once I had decided which of them to keep. I was sure that Aridar would help me choose then maybe even buy the other one for herself.

But what to do with the pair in the meantime? They would have to be kept somewhere although I couldn't imagine where as I headed home. There were rooms spare or even the cellar but they would have to remain chained until I needed the use of them.

By the time I reached my door I had decided that they would live under the house within easy reach should I need their assistance. First however I really wanted to discover the thrill of whipping them with my husband's old horse whip but I knew that I could not deal with them on my own.

Thinking on my feet I locked them into a large cupboard before going to see if Aridar was around to give me a hand. I met my tall blonde friend as she was coming back from the auction, livid that she had not been able to purchase anything for herself.

"The whole place has gone mad, Felani," she cried in frustration. "They were bidding stupid prices for these Roman dogs!"

"Don't worry, Aridar my dear," I said soothingly. "They

gave me a couple to play with because of what happened to Xavier."

"Of course, I was forgetting you poor thing," said Aridar, her eyes suddenly alive to the possibilities for the pair of us. "Where are they now?"

"They're locked up back at my place but I came to see if you would help me to deal with them," I replied.

"Well, I don't know," said Aridar mischievously, but after a pause for imaginary thought she screamed with excitement, "of course I will; let's get on with it!"

It only took a few moments for us to get back to my house with Aridar leading the way, her gorgeous bottom bobbing about ahead of me. Aridar had no partner but I knew that men lusted after her perfect body with its seemingly endless curves.

We found the slaves cowering in the darkness of the cupboard having made no obvious attempt to escape. These men were clearly cowed by the taste of defeat with the fight beaten out of them by the Dacian victors.

"These two are lovely," exclaimed Aridar as I dragged the pair from their temporary cell. "I was ready to hate these rats but they are too attractive to despise."

"Yes, but not too attractive to punish for what they have done to our people," I said firmly before we both lost our heads.

"Absolutely not," said Aridar hastily. "Let's teach them that Dacian women can be just as hard as Dacian men!"

"How are we going to do it?" I enquired not having the first idea how to administer a beating.

"Well, let me tell you what I once saw the priestesses doing to a couple of the virgins down in the temple," confided Aridar knowing full well that the slaves were listening to her intently.

Aridar explained that in order to maintain discipline amongst the young girls at the temple the priestesses often had to meat out severe punishments to some as examples to the rest. On one such occasion two of the girls had been singled out for such treatment even though they were innocent of any wrong-doings.

They had been strung up with their arms up their backs so that their buttocks were totally exposed to the priestesses' dreadful lashes. The girls had sung like larks as they were beaten but the priestesses ignored their pitiful pleas for mercy as they slashed away at their untainted flesh.

"So that is what we should do, except these boys actually deserve everything that we are going to do to them," said Aridar nodding towards the cowering slave boys huddled against the wall.

"Alright then, but you had better show me what to do," I conceded, willing to try out her plan.

As the slaves both had their wrists chained behind their backs already it was a relatively simple task to attach lengths of rope from my husband's old stores to the links between the slaves' wrists. We then led them out into the garden where a couple of ornamental arches provided ample support for captive arms.

With each of the slaves we looped the rest of the rope over the branches before pulling down as hard as we could on the other side. This had the immediate effect of doubling the boys over so that their firm buttocks were helplessly displayed.

"Simple, but very effective," said Aridar admiring our handiwork.

"Yes, the priestesses must have hours of fun with those poor girls," I said.

As the exertions of binding the boys had worn us out we decided to have a drink in the shade of one of the other trees. We sat in comfort whilst the boys struggled in the growing heat of the day their ankle chains jingling merrily as they vainly searched for more comfortable positions.

"Ah, this is the life," mused Aridar dreamily watching our captives straining in the burning sun. "When we have these two properly trained we will never have to work again!"

"So you're planning to stick around are you?" I asked sarcastically.

"You bet; I wouldn't miss this lark for the world," she cried jumping to her feet. "And it's about time that we flogged these two within an inch of their lives, what do you think?"

"Yes, I suppose it is, " I replied reluctantly following her towards the squirming slaves.

Having wanted to whip these boys for what their countrymen had done I suddenly felt that it was wrong to make them suffer. They already looked as though they were suffering enough as it was with their arms harshly bound up behind their backs.

Aridar offered me the long leather horsewhip shiny from the years of loving oiling it had received from Xavier. It looked like a dangerous black snake writhing in her hands as she stroked it pensively with her strong fingers.

I shook my head not quite ready to follow Burebista's orders and extract the revenge from the captured soldiers that he wanted us to with lash. Instead I indicated that Aridar should go first which seemed to be exactly what she wanted.

She dashed over to where the two men hung in painful shame awaiting their fate. They were already moaning softly into their gags but I was sure that Aridar would soon cause them to make much more noise with skilful flicks of the whip.

I sat back down in order to watch the way Aridar flogged the slave boys in the hope that I too would be able to summon up the courage to take hold of the lash myself. I wanted to beat them but looking at their handsome faces already contorted with pain somehow held me back.

Aridar had no such reservations for she simply went up to

147

the nearest of the slave boys snapping the whip between her hands. Without any further hesitation she swung the singled thonged whip back behind her before slashing it forward with as much strength as she could muster.

A loud crack resonated around the garden as the leather impacted violently on the olive skin of the hapless Roman leaving an angry red line over his buttocks. The poor boy screamed into his gag as he involuntarily swayed forward clearly stunned at the ferocity of the blow.

Aridar was delighted with the effect of her first stroke so she quickly prepared for her next one as the lash whistled back behind her in one fluid movement. She looked so comfortable with the long whip in her hands that I wondered just how many times she had done this kind of thing before.

Once again the whip flashed forward at breathtaking speed to land on another selected part of the poor slave's flesh. This time a bright scarlet line appeared across the boy's muscular thighs causing him to whimper pathetically at the excruciating pain Adrian was introducing him to.

A third stroke caught the slave on his lower back which actually brought a tear of despair to his deep brown eyes for obviously he had never been treated this way before especially by a mere woman. His descent into his own personal hell was almost complete but there was nothing that he could do to prevent Aridar compounding his shame with more strokes.

"This is fantastic, " cried Aridar as she lashed away at the poor boy another time.

"Yes, you look as though you are enjoying yourself," I responded hiding the surprise at her expertise in my voice. "Have you ever done this before?"

"Many times," replied Aridar casually lining up another stroke with the whip. "I used to live with a girl who loved having this done to her all the time."

"My, you have lived," I said astonished at this revelation. "You never told me that you were that way inclined!"

"Oh yes, I'll try anything as long as it leads to a good orgasm," said Aridar cheekily. "And speaking of which, beating this boy has got me all excited!"

I looked at her with what must have been an incredulous expression on my face because Aridar stopped in mid-lash to explain herself.

"You know, between my legs!" she said looking me straight in the eye. "When I used to whip Felicia I enjoyed it as much as she did and my sex always became wet with the thrill of it all."

"So what did you used to do about it?" I was amazed to hear myself asking.

"Well, I used to release the girl from whatever painful position I had tied her in, except for her wrists bound behind her back and ordered her to get to work between my legs," said Aridar mysteriously.

"Why, my dear, whatever do you mean?" I enquired still none the wiser.

"You have led a sheltered life, haven't you?" she replied walking back to my side her eyes shining bright with mischief. "What I mean is I made her lick between my beauty lips with her lovely long tongue."

"You mean she actually..."

"Yes, she pushed her tongue deep into my soaking pussy and lapped her way to some of the best orgasms I have ever had," she breathed almost into my ear.

I shivered with excitement as I experienced the first proper tingles of sexual arousal since Xavier had been cruelly taken from me. This naughty scamp was actually telling me how another woman had brought her forbidden pleasure between her legs with her tongue.

I found the idea both repulsive as well as highly stimulating at the same time. I could feel my nipples hardening through the thin material of my nearly diaphanous robes to the extent that it was becoming difficult to fight the urge to beg Aridar to perform the same service for me.

"Pass me the whip then," I said hastily taking the re-coiled instrument of correction from the minx's hands.

I needed to distract myself from this girl's attentions so I strode over to the other of the slave boys who had seen the wicked attention his comrade had been receiving. He tried to pull away from me looking terrified at the prospect of experiencing some of the same treatment.

I knew that I had to work some of this unwanted sexual energy out of my system so I simply moved next to the struggling boy where I raised the whip above my head. With no thought as to the direction of the stroke I brought the lash down across his unprotected skin as quickly as I could.

I was shocked to see the crimson gash that I had produced appearing before my eyes over the tender flesh of his buttocks. I was also ashamed to hear the boy moaning loudly into his gag as he tried in vain to get away from me but there was also something very arousing about wielding the whip over this helpless young man.

With a deeply satisfying thwack I slashed the whip down over the boy's buttocks once again enjoying an overwhelming sensation of having the ultimate power over him. With no skill or discernment I lashed the poor boy until he was covered with the long red marks left by a very busy whip.

"That was your first time, wasn't it?" asked Aridar when I finally put the whip down.

"Yes, how did you know," I responded still panting with all the exertion.

"Well just look at all those red lines everywhere," said Aridar pointing to the slave boy's body.

"I see what you mean," I said feeling guilty at the criss crosses of havoc I had wreaked over the boy's flesh.

"But I bet you enjoyed it though didn't you?" cried Aridar spying my rock hard nipples almost bursting through my garments.

"Yes...I suppose I did," I stammered trying to hide the evidence of my arousal by clumsily covering my breasts.

"Don't be embarrassed about it because I am still as wet as a waterfall after my adventures with the whip," confided Aridar sliding over to me. "And I know exactly what to do about it."

"But I don't think that I could..."

"Not with me, silly," said Aridar as if reading my mind. "At least not yet anyway!"

"Well, with who then?" I asked.

"Who do you think?" she replied looking over at the two slave boys.

"You don't mean..." I said following her gaze already considering the possibilities.

"They are yours to do with as you please so you might as well make them work for us," my friend said reasonably.

"But I thought we were just supposed to punish them," I said feebly attempting to combat my growing desire.

"Burebista would want you to get pleasure out of them as well," insisted Aridar.

"But what about..." I said helplessly.

"And Xavier wouldn't mind, I'm sure," said Aridar persistently, again guessing my thoughts. "After all he would want you to be happy even though he has gone."

She had hit the nail on the head, for thoughts of Xavier were filling my head. I knew it would be disloyal to his memory to use these boys in such a way but I had been faithful to his memory for so long. There is only so much of that a girl can take before she has to give in to her wanton desires.

In the end I did give in to the designs of the scheming Aridar who could hardly wait to get her hands on one of the slave boys. As soon as I consented she bounded over to the one that she had beaten in order to release the rope holding his wrists up his back.

As the freed rope slid over the bar above him the slave boy fell to the ground at Aridar's feet groaning in pain as well as relief. But he did not have long to recover for Aridar had work for him to do.

"Up you get, my beauty," she said dragging him to his feet by pulling sharply on his short black hair.

Aridar wandered over to our comfortable chairs with him hobbling along behind her, his ankle chains impeding his progress somewhat. I followed the pair taking the chance to admire the boy's legs as he followed his new mistress as quickly as he could.

He had obviously marched hundreds of miles on those fine, tanned legs for his muscles rippled with power each time he took a faltering step. I felt a pulse of excitement between my legs at the inescapable image of him working on my thoroughly aroused sex.

I watched enthralled as Aridar sat on her chair with the totally compliant slave boy kneeling submissively before her. Without any shame at all Aridar lifted the hem of her long flowing dress before beginning to pull it slowly up her beautiful long legs which she had spread obscenely wide apart in a most unladylike fashion.

As the dress retreated across her creamy coloured thighs it soon became apparent that she was not wearing any undergarments at all. The short blonde hairs of her neatly trimmed bush appeared at the top of her legs barely hiding her pouting beauty lips which were already well coated with the dew of her arousal.

"Now then, young man, let's see what Romans boys can do

with their tongues," whispered Aridar deftly undoing the boy's gag which slipped from his mouth wet with his saliva.

The former Roman sergeant opened his mouth to speak, completely thrown by this latest challenge in his career.

"No, I did not give you permission to speak," said Aridar firmly. "I want you to use your tongue for better thinks than talking."

With that she grabbed the boy's hair again this time thrusting his face between her thighs making her intentions even more obvious.

It was amazing to see that this comely but slender girl have total authority over this brutal Roman soldier. He was at least twice her size but she handled him as though he were a wayward puppy in need of some firm direction.

"That's a good boy, now just put your tongue in there," she said encouraging her new toy. "Ooh, that's perfect, carry on doing that until I allow you to stop."

I could see the boy's head bobbing up and down between Aridar's spread thighs but could only really guess exactly what he was doing to her. Whatever it was Aridar seemed to be enjoying it immensely as it wasn't long before she was moaning with delight.

Eventually her whole body began to undulate in time with the boy's efforts making her firm young breasts wobble delightfully under her robes. Her moans grew louder as the stimulation increased until finally she threw her head back screaming with pleasure.

It seemed to take ages for the girl to come back down to earth again especially as the slave boy continued to work away regardless of the state of his mistress. When she had recovered a little Aridar looked at me with the dreamy eyes of a girl who had just had the time of her life.

"That was even better than whipping this wretch," she cried

pulling the boy's head from between her thighs to withdraw his exploring tongue. "Your turn to have a go."

"I don't really think..." I said.

"Don't be ridiculous," Aridar interrupted. "What this boy lacks in technique he more than makes up for in enthusiasm and you know you want to find out what it feels like!"

"Well I suppose I could," I murmured, my defences crumbling with every faltering word.

"That's a good girl," said Aridar resolutely. "Now get yourself over here and lift that gorgeous dress of yours up like I have."

"Alright, but I'm not sure about this," I said as reluctantly as ever.

"Of course you're not; none of us are to start with but you'll love it, I promise!" my friend said earnestly.

I sat myself down in the spare chair before slowly peeling my dress and my undergarments back up my legs. I didn't think that my legs were quite as sexy as Aridar's but they were still shapely and were still admired by male friends.

"Ok, boy, you know what to do now so get over there and do the same for your owner or else," warned Aridar shoving the boy in my direction with her sandalled foot.

As he approached me I could see that his face was covered with the juices from Aridar's pussy. He had obviously been working very hard for her but his eyes were still frightened no doubt at the prospect of another whipping if he failed to please me in any way.

Behind those eyes however I detected a glimmer of excitement at what he was about to do which was backed up by the fact that his penis was now rock hard. Whilst Aridar had whipped him I could not help but notice that his cock had remained flaccid but as soon as he had begun to serve Aridar it had grown to an impressive size indeed.

This boy clearly didn't like being whipped by women but he certainly loved to satisfy them. As if to reinforce this he smiled briefly before lowering his noble head between my thighs which were now as stretched apart as Aridar's had been previously.

How easily I was slipping into the role of mistress over this boy who was so willing to please me. I jumped slightly as the boy's tongue brushed against the auburn bush on its way to previously uncharted territory. It still intrigued me as to exactly how he was going to pleasure me but as he skilfully parted my already wet labia with his tongue, his intentions soon became clear.

The boy's tongue darting inside my sex was the most exquisite feeling I had ever experienced to the extent that my head started to spin. I raised my hips to meet his eager lapping which meant that I was soon moving in time with his head below me.

Shivers of joy flooded through my body as his tongue penetrated deeper up into my vagina but I wanted more so I grabbed his hair as Aridar had done. This allowed me to dictate his actions to my meet my needs so he actually became my sex toy as he worked away inside me.

With one last pull of his head towards my gaping sex I came with a ferocity that I had not encountered since Xavier and I had first been lovers. I cried out totally gripped with lust, for this boy had turned me into some sort of rapacious beast who couldn't get enough of his attentions to my most intimate of places.

Once I had climbed down from that great high I pushed the boy gently aside to giver him the chance to get his breath back. I now realised exactly what Aridar had meant about the boy's experience and passion although it seemed to me that he knew precisely what he was doing.

"You enjoyed that too, didn't you?" laughed Aridar coming over to stroke my hair as I lay in my chair recovering form my shattering orgasm.

"I did; thank you," I replied extremely embarrassed at what I had done.

"Hasn't he been a good little boy," said Aridar patronisingly to the boy who was now cowering on the floor obviously afraid of the girl who had whipped him so mercilessly.

"Well, he certainly satisfied me!" I said laughing loudly at having been so wanton.

"So what do we do with them now?" asked Aridar looking over at the other one still hanging in his bonds.

"I supposed they need feeding don't they although I have no idea what you feed a slave boy these days," I replied shrugging my shoulders.

"I think that we should give them our leftovers so let's eat then make them clean up our scraps."

"Oh, Aridar, you are a naughty girl, aren't you," I playfully admonished her.

Before we went off to have a leisurely lunch together in the cool of my kitchen Aridar persuaded me to help her string the freed slave boy back up like his companion even though he had worked so hard for us. Aridar claimed that we needed to secure him to ensure peace of mind as we shared lunch together.

Once he was back in his painful place we went off to discuss mundane matters such as the latest fashions in Dacia. Whilst we chatted away the two slave boys continued to suffer in the increasing heat of the day, which made me feel very odd yet strangely elated at having such power over them.

"You know, we should name them," said Aridar as she sipped her red wine made from grapes grown on the banks of the distant Danube.

"Whatever do you mean; I'm sure that they have names of their own," I retorted surprised at her latest proposal.

"Yes, but we own them now so we have the right to call them what we want," said Aridar reasonably.

"Well what do you recommend we call them?" I said smiling at the idea that we now both possessed the slave boys.

"I was thinking of Romulus and Remus," said Aridar unaffected by the slight sarcasm in my voice. "After all they are from Rome and they look a little like twins."

"If you insist, but as they do look alike how will we distinguish them?" I asked.

"I believe that slaves are branded as a way of identifying them and of proving ownership," said Aridar undeterred by the look of horror on my face.

I had not thought of branding the slave boys but Aridar was right in saying that this was what happened to slaves in Dacia and in Rome. I tried to tell her that I would have no part in it but she was so insistent that I found myself listening to the details of how it would be done.

Before I knew what was going on we had let Romulus and Remus down then locked them still chained in the cupboard where I had left them earlier in the day. It seemed that they would have to wait even longer for the crumbs that we had left for them.

We then hurried down the street to the local blacksmith's where we purchased two metal bars with letters welded to the end that were usually used for branding cattle.

Because we had decided during the meal that Aridar would control one slave and me the other we agreed that hers would have an 'A' emblazoned on his skin whilst mine would have a bold 'F' for Felani.

Once we were armed with the branding bars as well as information as to the best way to brand animals we set off back to my home to feed our slaves. It was very exciting to think that we would soon brand the boys as ours forever and I was more than happy to share my good fortune with Aridar who was turning out to be an expert on dealing with slaves.

Back in the house we released the boys from the cupboard so they could see what we had purchased especially for them. They didn't look too grateful at what we were going to do for them but we still decided to feed them anyway.

Aridar gleefully spread the tiny pieces of bread left over from our lunch on the cold hard tiles of the kitchen floor. She then pulled the gags out of the boys' mouths who fell thankfully to their knees in order to eat up the bread as best they could.

I watched in amazement as the boys scurried around the floor trying to lick up every morsel of bread even trying to push each other out of the way. They must have been starving to abase themselves in this way but they did not seem to care how they looked, grovelling at the feet of their mistresses.

"I think that they would probably appreciate a drink as well, so let's see how they deal with these," said Aridar placing two bowls of water near to the struggling slaves boys.

Instantly they shuffled over to the bowls in order to bend over with their parched tongues sticking out. They both lapped up the water like dogs as best they could, spilling most onto the floor as they tried to quench their thirst.

"My, you were thirsty boys," said Aridar as if she were talking to two errant children. "Now make sure you clean up the mess on the floor as well or Mistress Aridar will be very cross with you both."

The boys flew into a flurry of activity as they tried to avoid further beating by licking the floor clean of all the crumbs and water that had been strewn before them. The floor was absolutely spotless by the time they ceased their frantic activity but

Aridar was still keen to pick fault.

"You call that clean, you snivelling excuses for men," snarled Aridar as meanly as she could. "You're going to pay for this slack behaviour but first we are going to brand the pair of you to confirm that you are truly ours to do with what we will!"

The two slave boys shrank away from her but she signalled to me to help her gag the boys again before dragging them back out to the garden. Once there we bound the pair with their backs to two trees using the same rope as before, leaving them utterly helpless.

They were still chained up under the rope but we spread their thighs as far as they would go with yet more rope. This made the inside of their muscular thighs which were the intended targets for our branding irons clearly visible.

"Help me set up your brazier up out here then we'll sit and watch them sweat as the coals heat up," said Aridar tripping off back to the kitchen.

It seemed now that Aridar was totally in control of the situation and that I was simply her assistant. Still I was following the orders of our glorious leader Burebista as well as enjoying myself at the slave boys' expense.

We soon had the coal burning brightly in the brazier which we had placed in front of the boys where they could see their fate unfolding before them. Back in the shade we sat drinking lime juice whilst watching the boys' faces distort in horror as the two branding irons slowly changed colour signalling their approaching readiness for use.

I still had grave reservations about marking the boys in this way but Aridar was insistent that this was the done thing. So, when the letters were glowing white hot, Aridar walked over to the brazier staring at her two trembling victims.

"Alright Felani dear, which one do you want?" she asked as she checked the letters in the glowing coals.

"Well, I think that I'll have the one who served us so well," I was surprised to hear myself say.

He had already proved himself on his knees so I thought that I would take him whilst Aridar trained the other one up to her obviously high standards.

"Very well, so I shall have this one," she replied.

Both boys looked absolutely terrified as Aridar started to rotate the branding irons in the fire to ensure that they were hot enough.

"These are ready for action now, Felani," she said beckoning to me to go over and join her by the brazier.

"Look, I'm not sure about this..." I said.

"You weren't sure about the flogging or the licking, but I know you were glad you did it," said Aridar firmly. "Now brand your slave boy to prove your ownership and we can get on with enjoying them so more!"

"Alright, but you first and show me how it's done," I said.

Without a second thought Aridar lifted the white hot 'A' iron from the coals and proceeded to manoeuvre it towards her target's immobilised thigh. The boy struggled in his bonds but he was doomed, for try as he might he could not escape.

"Keep still because you wouldn't want me to make a mess of this, would you?" snarled Aridar through gritted teeth of concentration.

The boy shook his head then remained as motionless as he could given what was about to happen to him. His eyes were wide with horror as the burning iron approached the hitherto flawless skin of his right thigh.

With a faint hiss the branding iron made contact with the boy's flesh causing him to scream piteously into his gag especially as Aridar held the scorching letter against him for several seconds.

When she was satisfied that the brand was clear enough

she took the iron away leaving a perfect 'A' of the deepest angriest red. The poor boy took one look at the iron as it was pulled away then fainted at the pain overwhelming him.

"There, all done," said Aridar patting the unconscious boy's cheek.

"Oh, that must have been awful for the poor thing," I whimpered.

"He'll recover," said Aridar breezily. "Now it's your turn so come and do yours!"

Slowly I approached the brazier where my branding iron glowed evilly, waiting to bring agony to my slave boy. My hands were shaking as I picked up the metal rod which was cool by the handle but blistering at the business end.

I knew that I had to keep a steady hand or I would make a total mess of the boy's leg so I steeled myself to the task ahead. I could not look into his frightened eyes but instead concentrated on the patch of skin that was soon to bear my initial.

With as much care as I could I aimed the brand next to his leg then plunged it into the flesh for a few seconds keeping it absolutely still as Aridar had done. The boy screamed as loudly as his colleague had done but mercifully passed out quicker than he did.

I took the brand away then replaced it in the fire before going to sit beside my triumphant friend. I was shaking like a leaf so she plied me with a glass of wine to steady my nerves.

"You did well there, Felani," said Aridar admiringly. "Look, you have left an exquisite mark on him - he'll be proud of that one day."

I seriously doubted her words but it was true that the 'F' on the boy's thigh was strangely attractive in a brutal sort of way. It stood as a final testament to his transition from fearless soldier to humbled slave boy. My slave, my very own property, brought to me by my right as a Dacian widow.

161

As the boys were still unconscious we decided to leave them in their bonds to recover for a while whilst we discussed the names that we would give them. I was happy with Aridar's choice reflecting their similarity with each other and their Roman roots.

We decided that Aridar's slave boy should be called Remus as he had been chosen second so my charge would be called Romulus. Aridar would also move into a room in my spacious house whereas the slaves would sleep in their large cupboard unless they were needed in either of our beds.

That was even more shocking for me than what had gone before for I had never considered actually laying with another man since my beloved Xavier had been taken from me. But again Aridar insisted that it would be alright so we discussed in detail the limitless possibilities of having two such malleable slave boys.

I was so excited again when we had finished yet another bottle of wine that I wandered out with Aridar to see how the boys were doing. As we approached it was clear that they had come round for they were both whimpering into their gags with the constant aching of their new brands.

I walked up to Romulus to let him have the good news that he was now my slave as well as to share with him his new name. He didn't look very happy despite me explaining to him that he would never experience pain like the brand in future unless he really misbehaved.

As it was already evening Aridar and I agreed to leave the boys tied where they were for the night so that they wouldn't be tempted to interfere with their rapidly forming brands. We would retire for the night also but to the comfort of our beds after the excitements of the day.

"You don't expect me to sleep alone do you?" asked Aridar in a small scared voice.

Suddenly the brash young woman who had easily dominated the two slave boys looked like a frightened girl when faced with the prospect of a night alone. I couldn't believe that Aridar could change so suddenly for it had seemed that nothing would unsettle her at all.

"What do you suggest then?" I asked with a raised eyebrow.

"Well, we could sleep together, perhaps..." she whispered hopefully.

I thought for a moment about this bubbly blonde girl before me who was pleading with me to share her bed for a reason I couldn't begin to fathom. She was a child again, seeking reassurance in the strangeness of a cruel world expecting me to take on the role of guardian or mentor to guide her through the night.

Whether she was acting or not I will never know but she spent the entire night as naked as the day she was born in my arms. She was as content as a kitten with cream though I did nothing to her other than occasionally stroke her long yellow hair though the darkest hours.

It was clear that she was a troubled girl but when the morning came she was up with the larks as bright as a button. She breakfasted quickly then rushed out to wearing only a diaphanous robe to see how Romulus and Remus had fared during the night.

I followed behind but by the time I reached the trees that had ensured the boys suffered a long sleepless night Aridar had already undone the ropes holding Remus. He fell to the floor in an exhausted heap with his chains still rattling around him.

"Poor boy needs to sleep, don't you Remus, but he has work to do," she said half sympathetically, half evilly.

Long gone was the fearful maiden of the previous night

replaced by a self confident dominatrix who knew exactly what she was going to make Remus do for her. He was her slave boy there to serve her in any way she chose and she was going to start with more sexual stimulation.

She rolled Remus over onto his back with his body weight resting on his manacled wrists before straddling his head with his naked body stretched in front of her. She parted her robes so that she could lower her sex directly onto his upturned face.

"Now to train this one like that other one," said Aridar with a dreamy grin.

She began to jerk her hips forward which meant that her sex rubbed against Remus' mouth. By stroking his lips with hers she was inviting him to serve her as his colleague had done but it did not seem as though he wanted to play along.

Undeterred Aridar leant forward in order to grab Remus' cock which was already starting to harden despite the boy's discomfort. Slowly she rubbed it fully to life whilst thrusting her beauty lips into his face still trying to tempt him into serving her.

As he still would not serve her with his tongue Aridar grabbed his testicles firmly in her hands before slowly squeezing them. She was determined to make Remus work for her one way or another and it seemed that it was working.

Aridar began to rock gently on his face as well as moan softly in response no doubt to Remus' tongue. Her face was a picture of contentment as she rode her slave boy towards her first orgasm of the day her hands still gripping Remus' balls to encourage him to work even harder for her.

Remus' cock was still fully erect, betraying the fact that he was enjoying himself but Aridar did not repay the favour. She did not even touch his penis despite the fact it rose temptingly before her like a mini colossus.

A brief cry of joy signalled that Aridar had come but she

remained exactly where she was with her dripping sex pressed down on Remus' face. For a brief moment she cut off his air supply completely to reinforce the notion that she possessed him now from the food he ate to the air he breathed.

Eventually Aridar climbed off her charge then ordered him to walk over to the house for breakfast leaving me to release Romulus from his tree. The poor boy looked absolutely exhausted but I noticed that he was as erect at the possibility of giving me the same pleasure as Remus had given to Aridar.

I did not fancy following Aridar's example out in the open so I too told my slave to go into the villa but not for the bread that Aridar was making Remus eat off the floor.

Instead I took him to my room where I lay back on my bed before shamelessly grasping my ankles. This not only threw my thin night-clothes open but also laid bare my hopelessly excited sex as an open invitation to Romulus to serve me.

As I had removed his gag on the way to the house the boy crawled eagerly between my lewdly spread thighs panting with desire. He obviously enjoyed the taste of my juices which were flowing freely from my over-excited sex.

With no hesitation this time he plunged his tongue between my beauty lips to savour my nectar which made me start to moan with enjoyment almost immediately. As he explored the depths of my vagina I writhed around in total abandon.

He had been a quick learner under the guidance of Aridar for he soon drove me to the edge of ecstasy with his insistent probing. I did not have to grab his hair as she had though for he seemed to sense the little extra effort that was required on his part.

With a determined lunge of his tongue Romulus sent me to heaven accompanied by a wild chorus of my own cries of joy. I had never known such happiness at the hands of a man for even my beloved Xavier had not been such a skilful lover.

165

Once I had calmed down again I looked down to see Romulus' smiling face practically drenched in me juices. Like a naughty school boy he licked his lips then winked at me for he realised what effect he had just had on me.

Much as I hated the very thought of it I was falling for this boy, this enemy of my people. It was becoming extremely hard to treat him the way Burebista wanted us to but I knew that I had to do something to make him suffer for the things his army had done to my people.

I decided to take him back to the kitchen so that I could ask Aridar's advice for she would surely know what to do. She did not let me down for as our two slave boys ate their breakfast of bread and water off the floor she told me about what had happened to the last lot of Roman prisoners brought back to the Dacian capital.

Aridar told me that some of the captured soldiers had been reduced to the level of pets of the rich women of Dacia. This meant that some of them lived literally as dogs which inevitably needed to be taken for walks in the local parks.

It had become the height of fashion to take out a handsome slave boy as a dog on all fours complete with collar and lead. Many high-class ladies were seen in the local public parks with their slave dogs at their heels obediently accompanying their mistresses on their morning constitutionals.

We decided that we would resurrect this idea whether it was still fashionable or not for it would be a good outward sign of our contempt for our Roman slaves. Secretly we could deal with them at home how we wanted but at least other Dacians would see them paying their debts to our society.

Once breakfast was over Aridar told me how the slaves were prepared for their walks in the past so that we could copy the same style. There were things that we needed from the local stores to do the job properly so I furnished Aridar with

166

funds to go and get them whilst I set the slaves to work around the villa.

The boys had not had their hands freed from behind their backs since I had seen them being dragged into Sarmizegethusa the day before. I could not risk releasing both of them so I locked Remus in the cupboard before chaining Romulus' ankle to the foot of my bed.

"Now, I am going to swap the chains on your wrists from back to front and I don't want any funny business, boy!" I said as firmly as I could. "Or else I will leave you chained here until Aridar gets back then we'll thrash you to within an inch of your life, do you understand?"

"Yes, Mistress," he said, his head bowed in total submission.

It was the first time that I had heard the boy speak and his soft dulcet tones made me shiver with passion. Not only was he gorgeous but he had the soft voice of an angel and it took all my willpower to prevent myself from falling at his feet in adoration.

To take my mind off this Adonis before me I busied myself with transferring his chains as I had promised. I allowed him to briefly rub his chafed wrists prior to rebinding his hands in front of him with the sturdy manacles.

Once he was secure I ordered him to start cleaning my house from top to bottom. I had previously employed a maid to do the housework but I found it much more interesting to watch Romulus do the work for me in his chains without a stitch of clothing to hide his heavily muscled frame. I sat on one of my comfortable chairs so that I could observe his every move as he bent to sweep the floor or reached up to dust my shelves.

He looked absolutely magnificent as he dutifully followed every one of my commands. He even stood with his hands stretch high above his head for no other reason than me wanting to look at his bound subjugated body.

I could not believe that such a beautiful creature was in my power or that it had cost me nothing other than being the widow of a Dacian war hero. I still struggled with feelings of guilt over Xavier but life went on and I had been presented with an opportunity that I did not want to pass up.

I made him work quickly for I wanted to see his body glistening with the sweat of his labour. All the time he toiled away for me he sported a huge erection betraying his pleasure at being made to sweat for his new mistress. I found myself practically panting with lust as he moved around in front of me in his eager desire to please.

Unfortunately my private viewing of a slave boy at work was interrupted by the return of Aridar who was weighed down with various bags from her shopping expedition. I ordered Romulus to kneel at my side whilst I looked at the strange assortment of items that she had bought for us.

There were mostly leather objects with chains attached in her bags but I could not tell what they were all for until Aridar patiently explained their uses to me. I could tell that Romulus was listening as we discussed the purchases doubtless wondering how the contents of the back would affect him.

Aridar said that the best way to show me how the devices were used was to actually fit them so we decided that we would prepare Romulus as a dog before tackling Remus.

As the special bindings needed lots of lengths of rope we made Romulus bring them to us on his knees.

Aridar then proceeded to bind the still-kneeling slave's left wrist to the same arm with ropes wrapped round under his armpits. She repeated this with his right arm so that both arms were effectively folding back on themselves with his fingers flailing uselessly in the air.

Romulus' wrist manacles were then removed so that he could separate his arms but she wasted no time in encasing his hands into clenched fists within little black leather mittens. The mittens were laced up tight so that Romulus had no chance of freeing himself from them.

Once she was happy with his arms she made him lean forward onto the floor so that his upper body rested on his elbows. She then quickly pulled back his lower legs and tied them to his thighs with yet more lengths of rope wrapped meticulously around his legs.

This meant that his whole weight now stood on his knees and elbows which left him already dog-like in his bound submission. To allow Romulus easier mobility Aridar attached four leather pads to his knees and elbows with leather straps.

She wanted the boy to suffer but she did not want him to wear out his skin on the long walks she had planned for our new pets. The image was completed by a chain lead of about three feet in length which she clipped to Romulus' collar by which we would control him on our journeys outside.

With a confident air she repeated the same procedure on the cowering Remus whom she dragged blinking from the darkness of his cupboard cell. Before my very eyes she created her very own puppy dog which she would take out alongside mine.

We placed their gags firmly into their mouths for we did not want any unwanted noises from them in the park. They were not sufficiently trained yet but it wouldn't be long I was sure before they would be allowed out without gags in for we would teach them the doggy sounds that they would be allowed to make outside.

We left them in the hallway whilst we dressed ourselves in our finest silks to go out to take the early afternoon air in the local park. We wanted to look our best as we paraded with our slave dogs in the streets for it was necessary to create the right impression out in society.

When we were satisfied with our appearances we grabbed the leads of our respective slaves then lead them out into the road. We all looked magnificent as we strode along and I noticed that Romulus and Remus both had massive erections despite the obvious discomfort of their predicament.

Both boys walked as quickly as they could but we kept up a brisk yet stately pace as we moved through the city towards the park. I realised that people were looking at us as they passed by but none of them seemed in the slightest surprised at what they saw.

I was shocked at this until we reached the main park whereupon I saw many women leading similarly bound slave dogs sedately along the paths of the municipal park. Each slave dog was a former Roman soldier reduced to being a pet for his new owner by day then a sordid sex slave at night.

Aridar smiled as when she saw the look upon my face then led Remus off around the grounds with the other slave dogs. She was extremely proud of her slave dog so she was keen to show him off amongst the other ladies of society. I followed behind her occasionally looking down at Romulus who was panting into his gag beside me.

The whole thing seemed completely bizarre to me but I persevered with the walk until it was time to go home. We nodded to some of the ladies that we had met in the park before heading back up the street towards the villa.

"It looks like dog walking is back in fashion, Aridar my dear," I was amazed to hear myself say as if it were all perfectly normal.

"Yes I believe it is," replied Aridar matter-of-factly.

"Well, I'm glad you made it all possible for us, but now it's time to get these two back and get some use from them," I announced even more astonished at my cheek.

"I couldn't agree more," responded Aridar with a wink.

Later on, once we dragged our slave dogs back home I reflected upon the events of the last two days. I straddled the naked Romulus who was tied spread-eagled to my bed with his mighty, erect cock rising temptingly before me, and wondered whether I should allow him to enter me.

He had come into my life as a prisoner of war only the day before but I knew that I already loved him. I also desperately wanted his cock inside my aching sex but it still felt wrong to me that I should even contemplate sex with one of Xavier's enemies.

Even as I lifted myself over his towering manhood I was racked with doubts but as his penis entered my void I knew that I was lost. His cock filled my vagina completely and I found myself wondering whether Burebista would allow me to marry my newly found slave dog...

As I hung in the air I could feel the straps of my parachute digging into my crotch in the most peculiar way. It seemed to add to the excitement that I already felt at what our team was doing that night, particularly the way it rubbed incessantly between my legs.

I could not believe that despite the obvious danger of what we were doing I could feel so aroused by the nylon belt. It actually seemed to stroke my pussy through the thin material of my jump suit every time the wind blew me about.

It was rare that I ever wore underwear because my breasts were firm enough to support themselves and panties only slowed my lovers down. Tonight was no exception for even though we were making a particularly hazardous descent I still wore nothing under my clothes.

You never knew who you would come across even when pursuing the mysteries of the universe or unmasking conspiracies so it paid to be prepared. With my flaming red hair and my figure hugging apparel I had defused many tricky situations by letting various guards know that I was completely naked beneath my suit.

As the ground rushed up to meet me I began to wonder what kind of guards would be waiting for us this time. I had lost count of the places I had been escorted from after being handcuffed then frisked but I had a real sense of foreboding about this one in spite of the sexual stimulation these trips always stirred within me.

I landed perfectly then rolled over as I had many times before gathering up the blackened canopy as quickly as I could. It was essential to be discreet or we would be captured long before we found out anything useful.

Once I had gathered my things together I hurried over to

where Tia, Richie and Bob were sorting themselves out.

"Everybody alright?" I whispered in the darkness.

"Yes, Sandy, we're all fine," Bob replied.

Bob was a tall, dark, handsome boy who had drafted me into all this top secret conspiracy stuff a couple of years before. He was strong and fearless which meant that he usually led us into some pretty hairy places.

This time it was the big one - a fortified base set up in the middle of a wilderness by a disenchanted general who had gathered to him many of the soldiers that had been under his command to form his own private Militia. Not only that but he had also acquired heavy weapons and even missiles. Not even the government knew what he intended for no unauthorised personnel were supposed to enter on pain of something which would be very nasty indeed. But these kinds of vague threats never put Bob off and he was determined to look behind the razor wire of this most top secret facility.

That was why he and I plus two of his other 'conspiracy' buddies made our way across the hard stony floor towards what he assumed was the centre of operations. We continued walking for about half an hour before we saw some lights in the distance.

They were clearly headlights racing towards us so Bob told us to run yet I knew that our game was already up. Our para-chutes had been spotted. We tried to hide but helicopters appeared above us like angry hornets shining their searchlights over the barren ground.

Swiftly we were captured by soldiers of the Militia in full combat gear who were even rougher with us than other guards had been in our previous encounters. I was shoved face down over the hood of a jeep before having my legs brutally kicked apart.

I felt the inevitable cold click of handcuffs on my wrists

prior to the sergeant liberally feeling up my legs through the thin material. I always felt a thrill when this happened to me for I knew that I was in the hands of a person with an authority and power that I could not resist.

His gloved hands skilfully assessed whether I was carrying any weapons or cameras by exploring every inch of my body. He lingered far too long as they all did on my full breasts and between my legs where I was already on fire with the flame of uncontrollable lust.

All very predictable until I heard my guard say," Miss Bossy Pants will love this one - she's wet through already!"

I jumped nervously when I heard this for I wondered what he meant. I had been interrogated many times before by people who had enjoyed their job. They loved having young girls like me at their mercy but nothing had ever actually happened to me.

But this man seemed to be hinting that something would be different this time and that the person responsible would really get a kick out of it. I was very tense yet still aroused as I was bundled into the back of the sergeant's jeep.

We were all transported in separate vehicles in the same direction in which we had been walking. At least Bob was going to see what was at the centre of the camp although I was becoming more worried the further in we went.

Eventually we came to a group grey buildings huddled beside what looked like a huge runway in the grey light of pre-dawn. The jeep pulled up sharply outside one of the buildings whereupon I was pulled out by my hair then dragged towards an ominously open door.

I could not see where my friends were being taken for I was whisked down a seemingly endless corridor then thrust into a tiny room. They pushed me in before locking the door behind them leaving me in the semi-darkness of my cell.

There was no window but light still filtered through the thick mesh which covered a small hatchway in the sturdy door. I could see that there was nothing else in the room so I wandered over to the far corner and sat down.

As they had not bothered to remove my handcuffs I slithered down the wall then attempted to make myself as comfortable as I could. They had already been rough with me yet something told me that things could only get worse.

I waited for what seemed like hours huddled on the cold hard floor of my cell thinking of all the things that might happen to me. I began to work myself up into a frenzy of fear until suddenly the door burst open flooding the tiny room with the glare of harsh strip lighting.

In the doorway was the silhouette of a woman with what looked like a riding crop in her hand. She stood with her legs apart and her hands on her hips like the very model of a stern prison guard.

"Up you get, you lazy bitch," she shouted. "It's time to find out what the hell you were up to out there in the desert!"

I tried to get up as quickly as I could but it was difficult with my hands still chained so she grabbed my hair by way of assistance. She pulled me to my feet with no concern for the excruciating pain she caused me then shoved me out of the room.

She continued to push me down various corridors until we arrived at what turned out to be her office. She made me stand in front of her desk with my legs splayed apart whilst she luxuriated in her huge leather chair opposite me.

I could see that she was quite an attractive woman in her early thirties with short-cropped blonde hair. Her large breasts were practically bursting out of the blouse of her uniform whilst her long thighs were exposed as she crossed her legs under her short military style skirt.

175

"So, what is your name?" she asked in a cool interrogator's voice.

"Sandy Jones," I whimpered already terrified of this imposing woman.

"Sandy Jones, Miss!" she shouted.

"Sandy Jones, Miss," I stammered.

"What were you doing out there in the desert in the middle of the night?" she demanded curtly.

"We wanted to do a night jump but I guess we strayed from our intended flight path," I replied as confidently as I could under the circumstances.

This was the answer that all four of us had rehearsed in case of capture for we did not want to be discovered as 'conspiracy chasers'. It was obvious that the answer was rehearsed for the woman just laughed at my feeble attempts to cover our true intentions.

"My name is Sergeant Banton and I eat bitches like you for breakfast," she said disdainfully. "I know you are lying and pretty soon you're going to be begging to tell me the truth."

"But it is true; the pilot must have..."

"Don't mess with me, madam," she hissed nastily. "I know more ways to torture a woman than you've had hot dinners so start talking."

"The plane was obviously in the wrong place..."

"Right, that's it," said Banton pulling her drawer open and taking out a huge knife. "The fun starts here and believe me I'm going to enjoy every minute I spend torturing you."

As she advanced upon me brandishing her knife I remembered what the brutal sergeant had said about 'Miss Bossy Pants' and how she would 'enjoy me'. I shivered when I realised that I might already be in the possession of 'Miss Bossy Pants' especially as she seemed to be about to attack me with her blade.

Instead she began to hack away at my dark blue jump suit which simply fell apart under her slashing cuts. In a trice I was naked before her which left me feeling even more vulnerable especially with my hands still cuffed behind me.

"Now, we shall start again," said Banton returning to her comfortable chair. "Tell me what you were doing snooping around in the desert so close to this facility."

"I told you, our plane must have veered off course and dumped us far from where we were supposed to be," I insisted but with much less conviction than when I still retained the dubious protection of my clothes.

"So, you persist with this nonsense about unfortunate navigation problems do you?" asked Banton in a deceptively conciliatory tone.

"Well, it's the truth..."

"I have heard that story four times now," snapped Banton. "And I am getting mighty sick of it!"

"What do you mean?" I stammered.

"I'm going to show you what I did to your friends who told me exactly the same," said Banton once again getting to her feet.

Very reluctantly due to my state of undress I followed her from her office out into the grey corridors. There was no-one about but I was still worried that someone would see me naked as well as in handcuffs following this brutish woman like a little lost pup.

After what seemed like an eternity we reached yet another grey door which Banton burst through with all the authority of a woman on a mission. I followed meekly behind her glad to be off the main passageways out of public view.

Once I was inside the dimly lit room however I wished that I was back in my cell for what I saw chilled me to the bone. In the gloom that pervaded the large room I could just about make out three tormented figures that looked terrifyingly familiar.

Tia, Bob and Richie had all been bound in various torturous positions before being left to their fate for the remainder of the night. Each one was heavily gagged to reduce the sounds they made as they suffered in their bonds but each looked forlornly at me with uncovered eyes.

"What have you done to them?" I cried in horror at what I was seeing.

"I dealt with this one first because I thought she would crack quickly," said Banton pointing at the distraught Tia. "But she stuck to her story so I bound her here so as I could be free to start on the other two."

Poor Tia had been strung up from the high ceiling with what looked like wire wound around her thumbs. Her long slender legs had been spread widely apart then secured with wire so that she was on tip toe.

She too had been stripped naked then yet more wire had been pulled up between her pussy lips then tied to a narrow belt around her waste. She looked like she was in complete agony because the wire appeared to be cutting her in two.

I felt desperately sorry for my friend but Banton moved on to where Richie was struggling in his confinement.

"This one was just as stubborn so I left him like this to see if it would help him change his mind," explained Banton looking down at her next victim.

Banton had hung him upside down by his spread ankles with his head a few inches from the floor. His wrists then his elbows had been bound together with wire which had then been dragged between his butt cheeks then attached to the beam that held his ankles.

It had been drawn so tight that his face actually looked directly at the ground whilst his back was arched cruelly backwards. His cock hung limply between his legs showing the

178

extent of his discomfort but his moans were lost in the folds of his heavy leather gag.

"Then there's this one," went on Banton. "He was actually rude as he lied to me so he's suffering more than the others already."

I wrenched my eyes from Richie to look at my lover who was squirming in the corner of the room. I could see that Banton had done a thorough job on him.

Bob had been tied spread-eagled on the unforgiving floor again with wire but what made his predicament awful was what Banton had done with his balls. She had wrapped wire several times round the base of his genitals then attached them to a long piece of wire that was fixed to a beam high above him.

Even in the gloom I could see all his muscles straining to keep his body up in order to relieve the pressure on his balls. Every few seconds his resolve would slip leaving most of his body weight dangling achingly from his throbbing scrotum.

"How could you do this to him?" I cried turning to our captor with tears in my eyes.

"People who don't answer my questions correctly get this sort of treatment and much worse until they do," snarled Banton. "And it's high time we selected a position for you to suffer in for the rest of the day!"

Banton was about to bind me into some awful position alongside my colleagues when she seemed to change her mind.

"No, I think that I will show you around a bit before I incarcerate you for the rest of the day," she exclaimed before pushing me back out into the corridor.

Once again she led me through never ending strip-lit passageways all of the same dull grey. We passed several soldiers on our journey who glanced appreciatively at me much to my great embarrassment.

It seemed that Banton wanted to humiliate me as part of the interrogation process and it was certainly working. The handcuffs prevented me from preserving my modesty so the soldiers feasted their eyes on my exposed body as they marched by.

Eventually we reached yet another door whereupon Banton knocked briskly then waited to be admitted. I stood beside her wondering what fresh horrors this door would reveal and shivering with nervousness in the bright glare of the corridor's lights.

"Come in!" shouted a gruff voice.

Banton pushed the door open then shoved me into what turned out to be a large plush office beyond. Another huge desk dominated the room but this time a middle aged man sat in the comfortable chair behind it.

"Ah, Banton, what have you brought me this time?" asked the self confident man in what looked like a high ranking officer's jacket.

"We found this bitch and her friends wandering around outside the camp after jumping into the area, sir," explained Banton nodding disdainfully in my direction.

"Plane went off course I suppose," said the officer drinking in my bound naked form with a well-practised eye.

"Of course, but I'll soon have the truth out of them, sir," replied Banton.

"I know you will Sergeant," said the officer. "And you'll have such fun doing it!"

"Yes, sir, I will," responded Banton again looking at me. "How are you getting on with that CIA slut I sent you after I'd broken her?"

"Oh fine, in fact she's down here doing her best to avoid being sent back to you," replied the officer with a huge grin across his face.

I had not noticed when I entered the room but under the

desk hidden partly by the drawers at either side was a naked girl on her knees. Her elbows and wrists had been bound together with wire and her lustrous black hair was piled up on the top of her head then secured with red ribbons.

I could see that her buttocks were covered with angry red lines which I could not explain but her face was hidden as her head was buried between the man's uncovered thighs. His trousers were round his ankles and it was quite obvious what the girl was doing to try to please him.

I heard slurping sounds coming from her mouth as she sucked his cock for all she was worth occasionally looking round to glance nervously at her audience. It was obvious from the look in her eyes that she did not really want to serve this man but that the consequences of failing to do so to the best of her ability were too dire to contemplate.

"Good General, I am glad to hear it," smirked Banton then looking at me again she continued. "Now this one has seen what can happen I am hoping that she will be more co-operative."

"Well, if not, you will have a whole heap of fun making her see it your way," said the General.

"Thank you for your confidence in me, sir," Banton replied.

Having made her point to me in that graphic way she saluted the general smartly before pushing me out of the room ahead of her. The implication was of course that I would end up like the poor CIA girl if I did not play ball.

As I walked before my tormentor down yet more passageways I considered coming clean so that I could avoid the kind of treatment I had seen her other prisoners receiving. If I told her of our obviously failed expedition she might let the four of us go with the usual reprimand thus avoiding any further pain for us all.

This seemed an attractive proposition especially as we seemed to be passing ever more highly interested soldiers who all ogled my body with hungry eyes. I did not want to end up being given to an officer as a plaything like the other poor girl had been.

I made up my mind to tell Banton everything when we reached the next scene of torture or humiliation that I was sure she had lined up for me. I would avoid whatever she intended to do to me by letting her have the information she seemed so desperate to know.

The next room that Banton took me to made me even more determined for inside it another girl was being subjected to horrors beyond my wildest nightmares. I simply could not believe what was happening to her or that her tormentors would stoop so low.

The petite brunette had been bent over a desk with her ankles and wrists secured tightly to each leg with strong cords. Her long brown hair had been plaited then attached to a rope that lead to a rafter above her forcing her head painfully upwards.

As if her plight were not bad enough but there were no less than three men in Air Force uniforms all tormenting her to their hearts' content. All three had their flies undone and sported massive erections as they happily carried out their tasks.

One stood in front of the hapless young woman with his penis deep in her mouth and his hands nonchalantly on his hips. He didn't move but expected the girl to do all the work as she sucked desperately for all she was worth.

Another stood at the side of the girl with his cock in his hands playing with himself. In his other hand he held a riding crop with which he was delivering vicious cuts across the girl's upper buttocks leaving long scarlet lines of agony.

The third stood behind the girl between her legs with his

member firmly planted inside her tortured body. He was thrusting away with great vigour but every time he pulled back I could clearly see the red gash of the girl's vagina below his emerging cock.

I was stunned to realise that he was actually pumping her anus as hard as he could whilst his balls bounced against her pussy where I logically thought his penis should be. The pitiful girl must have been in misery but bound as she was there was nothing that she could do to halt the ministrations of the three soldiers.

"Now then, boys, are you enjoying yourselves?" asked Banton with a wicked smile on her face.

"Yes, Sergeant," chorused the men not breaking off from abusing the girl.

"How long have you been playing with her like this?"

"Well, Sergeant, we've been taking turns to go round the table now for about an hour," said the man with the whip.

"But by the time we've each made the bitch swallow our come we'll all be ready to go again!" Said the one splitting her bottom with his determined lunging.

"And next time we might have to think of another place to shoot our loads," cried the last one as he appeared to come into the girls' mouth spurting his hot semen into the back of her throat until she gagged with it.

"Very good, boys, now keep up the good work," laughed Banton as she took one last look at yet another of her victims then led me down the corridor away from the scene of utter debauchery.

Banton did not bother to knock at the next door that we stopped outside simply pushed me threw it into another dimly lit room. As I quickly looked around the small room I could see that there were two metal frame beds along opposite walls with two identical metal cupboards next to them.

"Welcome to my little room which I share with a friend of mine, the delightful Sergeant Mires," explained Banton as she closed the door then turned on the overhead light.

"Why have you brought me here?" I asked nervously.

"It's my rest time now and you are here to help me enjoy myself," explained Banton sitting on her bed. "Mires will be along in a moment so the pair of us can have a little fun with you."

The General's little pet had made me think about surrendering but the desperate plight of the girl given to the mercy of those three soldiers convinced me of what I should do. The fact that any of the things that I had seen, or even worse, could happen to me made up my mind for me so I decided to capitulate at once.

"You've made your point, Miss; I give in, "I stammered. "I'll tell you everything you want to know."

"I know you will, you slut," retorted Banton wickedly. "But first you will serve Mires and me satisfactorily or else that last girl you saw will have a partner in her suffering!"

At that moment the door burst open to reveal another Militia sergeant with short black hair wearing an almost identical uniform to Banton's.

"Ah, Mires, there you are," exclaimed Banton. "Just look at what I've got for us to play with."

"I see you've excelled yourself this time," replied Mires as she surveyed my still bound form. "Looks even better than that slut you brought last time."

"Yes, but I think that this one is a little wet behind the ears so we will have to train her up a bit," Banton said disparagingly.

I felt my knees go weak as images of the girl on her knees in front of the General filled my mind. I vividly remembered her frightened eyes realising at that instant that mine would soon look exactly the same.

As I stood watching, the two women began to remove their uniforms piece by piece until they were down to their regulation hold-up stockings and highly polished court shoes.

"There now, we're all the same," said Banton condescendingly. "Except of course that you are now our slave and you will do precisely what we want you to or face the consequences."

"That's right, you little whore and I want you to start by setting that tongue of yours to work on my pussy," said Mires pointing between her legs. "It's hotter than hell down there and I need someone to stoke my fire!"

Mires laughed evilly as she lay back on her bed indicating what I should do for her by gently rubbing her labia. Her sex was completely shaved so it was easy for me to see that her lips were already moist with her excitement at having me as her new toy.

Hesitantly I climbed onto her tiny bed with her legs either side of me, which she had spread as wide as she could in readiness. The strong scent of her arousal filled my nostrils making my abhorrent task even more difficult especially as I had never served a woman in this way before.

Bob had suggested after a night of drunkenness with our friends that Tia and I should make out together. I was very much the worse for wear that evening but even though Tia was stunningly pretty as well as keen to try, I refused because I simply could not bring myself to do it.

Now I had no choice in the matter and that absolved me of all guilt so I steadied myself then lowered my head between her well-muscled thighs kept lady-like by the lacy tops of her silken hold-ups. Her lips pouted below my face like the cautiously opening petals of some strange exotic flower.

Suddenly the task didn't seem so bad, after all this was one of the things I shared with these overbearing women. It would not be so bad to lick this most beautiful of blooms so I leant forward in order to savour the nectar within her.

Slowly I stuck out my tongue until it touched the tender folds of flesh that hid the entrance to Mires' pink vagina. I pushed a little further beyond her lips then into the depths of her pussy which were soaked in a steady flow of her juices.

The taste was just as I had hoped for, as divine as any forbidden fruit that I had ever imagined in my wildest fantasies. It was quite delicious so I shoved my tongue deeper into her sex in an insatiable search for more.

I was deaf to her moaning below me as I worked my way inside her very being lapping every drop of her juices that I could. The violent shivers of her entire body were passed unnoticed for I was lost in a tempestuous sea of my own greed.

Lust overtook me so it was not until Banton dragged my head away from Mires' sodden gash by pulling my hair that I realised that Mires had come.

"Easy you slut, save some of that energy for me," cried Banton yanking my head back maliciously.

"My God, what a tart you really are," gasped Mires still recovering from the orgasm I had just engineered for her. "I thought you said she was shy and untouched."

"She is, or at least that's what she led me to believe," replied Banton lifting me off Mires' bed as easily as if I were nothing but a feather. "Perhaps the bitch was acting all coy to throw me off the scent."

"Either that or she's a damn quick learner," said Mires' getting groggily to her feet. "I have never been tongued like that before in all my life!"

"Well, she had better do the same for me or I'll string her up by her tongue," retorted Banton bitchily.

I knew that I had upset her somehow but I was not exactly sure how. Maybe it was because she thought she knew me already or perhaps I had served her little lesbian friend better than she ever had.

Either way she had it in for me because she decided to make it more difficult for me to pleasure her than Mires. She produced a heavy leather collar which she fastened around my neck as tightly as she could without actually strangling me.

She then pulled my handcuffed hands up my back before attaching them by the central link in the joining chain to a clip on the collar. This left me in a very awkward position having to hold my hands in place next to my shoulder blades to avoid choking myself.

"There, let's see if you're as good now, madam," said Banton coldly as she climbed onto her bed. "And if the bitch doesn't work as well as she did for you I want to you to thrash her cute little ass!"

"OK, Banton, whatever you say," said Mires as she went to retrieve an evil looking rattan cane from her cupboard.

It was clear who was in charge in their cosy relationship and I had obviously come back under the sway of the of the meanest of the pair. She would no doubt have me caned brutally for the slightest infringement of her rules so I hastily mounted her bed.

Once she had splayed her legs I obediently bowed my head in submission like a docile lamb to the slaughter. Her cropped pussy was not wet at all so I knew that I had my work cut out for me.

Immediately I set to work by skilfully parting Banton's labia with my tongue then licking upwards to find her clitoris shrouded in its fleshy hideaway. I pushed back the layers of skin to reveal her bud already hardening with my growing expertise.

I was just settling down to my task made difficult by the way I had been bound when I heard a sharp Crack! and felt a blazing sting across my buttocks. Apparently Banton had not been happy with my efforts for she had clearly directed Mires to beat me to persuade me to work even harder for her.

I began to lap at her clit as quickly as I could in the hope that Banton would be stimulated enough to stop having me caned. As I licked however another stroke of Mires' cane caught me on the soft flesh at the tops of my thighs.

It hurt so much that I attempted to get back up almost garrotting myself with the collar in the process. But Banton merely grabbed my hair so that she could force me back down on her gaping pussy stifling my scream of pain against her fleshy labia.

I could not fight against these women so the only thing I could do was to labour as hard as I could for the bitch that held me so tenaciously by my hair. A third biting stroke of Mires' cane spurred me into a blur of activity with my tongue darting into Banton's now wet quim like a ramrod.

It was fair to say that Banton's bittersweet tang was not as pleasant as Mires' but I soon began to crave the taste of my new mistress. More strokes fell across my burning cheeks but I no longer needed the encouragement of the cane as I toiled away between Banton's heaving thighs.

My tongue was soon all the way inside Banton's quivering vagina as I guzzled her juices for all I was worth. Occasionally I stopped my eager tongue in order to gently nibble her clit with my teeth as Bob had done to me countless time before. I knew that this had always driven me wild in bed so I hoped that it would have the same effect on Banton. It appeared that I had not hoped in vain for she started to groan loudly with delight and the frequency of the strokes of the cane seemed to abate.

After a few minutes of this sustained effort Banton experienced an orgasm that most have shuddered through her like an avalanche. She pulled my hair even tighter then her whole body went stiff as she reached her pleasure overload. It took quite some time for her to recover her self-composure once she had come for the aftershocks still rippled through her for some time.

I remained kneeling with my face still pressed up against her sex which was now ultra-sensitive following her crushing climax. Even the tiny involuntary moves I made sent Banton back into orbit as she could hardly bear to be touched.

"Wow, I know what you mean, Mires," sighed Banton finally as she drove me casually from her bed.

I nearly throttled myself again as I fell to the floor at the foot of her bed but she did not care for she was having a great deal of fun at my expense.

"Now get in the corner bitch so that Mires and I can get some sleep," Banton ordered me as if I was nothing more than a dog.

"Yes we're on nights again and we need our beauty sleep," agreed Mires.

"But doubtless we will have a use for you before we start our next shift," said Banton getting back onto her bed this time between her white starched sheets. "Now not another sound or I'll lock you in my cupboard while we get some shut-eye."

"Sleep well, slut" said Mires as she too made herself comfortable in her bed before turning the light out.

I was left to cower in the corner with my arms still chained agonisingly up my back far from contented as they were and even further from sleep. I heard myself whimpering in the darkness like a frightened child but forced myself to be silent to avoid further misery.

I realised that serving my new mistresses had actually turned me on but bound the way I was there was nothing I could do about it. I knew that my nipples were rock hard but I was not able to reach them. My pussy was also dripping with my own excitement but the chilly floor only served to douse my passion.

It was not long before I could hear the two women snoring softly leaving me wide awake with frustration at my plight. It would be a long wait for them to wake up to start their day and I didn't even know whether it was day or night any more. I had been captured at night but perhaps it was part of the general disorientation programme to rob me of any proper sense of time. Whatever their ploy it seemed to be working so all I could do was lie on my side in the forlorn hope that I would at least get some rest.

The hours dragged by as I drifted from being maddeningly awake to shallow cat-naps tortured by nightmares then back again to grim reality. I got to the stage where I thought I could not survive a moment longer then prayed for morning even though it would probably bring only more suffering for me.

Eventually when I was at my wits' end a bedside alarm went off rousing the two women from their deep slumbers. The light was snapped on practically blinding me before Banton made her way over to where I lay still racked in misery.

"Get up you lazy bitch because Mires and me have some more work for you to do for us," she shouted down at me.

Wearily I tried to get to my feet but found it impossible so Banton angrily heaved me up once again by my hair. I was absolutely worn out but I had the feeling that I knew what they wanted from me even though my mouth was still filled with their very distinctive tastes.

I prepared myself to eat the pair of them out again but they only wanted me to help wash and dress them for their busy day ahead. Once they had released the handcuffs from my collar then replaced them with my hands in front not behind they took me along to their communal showers.

There they had me soap them both down with sponges

then wash their hair with a shampoo that had a strange chemical odour. They were both very meticulous about their hygiene but neither seemed to be bothered about whether I was clean until they were both finished.

At this point they wrapped themselves in large white towels then snagged the chains of my handcuffs over a hook in the showers leaving me on tiptoe. Next they proceeded to play ice cold water across my body with a high pressure hose.

The water seemed to burn me as it slammed against my skin but the goose pimples covering my flesh proved just how cold the water was. They both thought it was hilarious the way I tried to jump about to avoid the freezing jet of water but the handcuffs kept me in place so they blasted the water all over me.

"Better spray the bitch's face to clean all trace of us off her," said Mires moving the hose up over my stiff nipples towards my head.

"Why bother," said Banton. "If she can taste us all day she will be reminded of all the things that we can make her do."

Mires agreed and mercifully turned off the hose pipe.

As they dried themselves off properly they left me to hang in my bonds still cold with water dripping from me. I was shivering uncontrollably but happier to have some of the previous day's grime blasted from my helpless body with the hose.

Once they had put on their fresh new uniforms with new stockings but no panties they decided to let me off my hook so they could take me along to breakfast with them with my hands chained behind me once again.

This was not so as I could reduced the pangs of hunger that had also plagued my night but so as they could gloat over me as they ate their food. I was made to kneel at the side of the small table they chose when they had selected all manner of wonderful items for their breakfasts.

"Are you hungry, you poor little thing?" said Banton sarcastically. "That's a shame because this chow is delicious."

"No she can't be hungry because she ate last night!" laughed Mires pointing to her crotch again.

"That's right my dear, so she did," sniggered Banton.

"Still I suppose we had better give her something else so she won't faint," said Mires looking down at where I knelt.

"Alright, but make the slut beg for it first."

"Here you are, you little bitch, here's a piece of sausage for you," said Mires.. "But you heard what the sergeant said, you'd better beg for it first."

"Please, Miss, may I have some food, I beg of you," I whispered humbly.

By this time I was starved enough to debase myself even further in front of these two sadists as well as all the other people in the canteen. Soldiers who were gathering for breakfast looked at me with great delight but I did not care, I just wanted food.

"Lick my shoes and I will consider it," said Mires winking at Banton.

Immediately I leaned forward in order to comply with her wishes so that she would feed me. I licked the patent leather of both women's shoes until they shined so desperate was I for sustenance.

When I had finished I knelt back up before repeating my plea for food, my eyes turned down as I guessed a submissive slavegirl's should be.

"Isn't that nice, the bitch is learning fast," said Mires not unpleasantly.

"Well, if you're so impressed give her the food," snapped Banton with a hint of jealousy in her voice. "But force her to suck it like a dick first!"

"OK, you heard the lady give it a good suck before you eat

192

it," ordered Mires holding out the sausage to me.

In front of a growing crowd of military personnel I sucked the sausage imagining it was Bobby's cock to help me give the impression I was sure they all wanted. I was slavering as I licked the tip of the sausage then slid it gently into my mouth like a good little girl.

My mistresses must have liked what I was doing for they both murmured their appreciation at my efforts. Once I had sucked most of the sausage into my mouth I took a bite which tasted absolutely delicious in my slightly emaciated state.

I chewed then swallowed the meat before resuming my show with the rest of the sausage that Mires still held out for me. After my noisy sucking I consumed the rest of the breakfast that I had earned with my grovelling humility.

Once Banton had finished her meal she took me away from the canteen with the laughter of the other soldiers ringing in my ears. They were obviously used to such displays of prisoner control by Banton there though it appeared that they had really enjoyed this particular demonstration.

I was taken to another room after what felt like a mile of corridors filled with yet more very attentive soldiers going about their business. None of them were surprised to see a naked girl with her wrists chained behind her being led through the base by Sergeant Banton.

Every time I saw another soldier, male or female I squirmed with embarrassment as their eager eyes seemed to burn into my very flesh. I tried in vain to cover myself but the handcuffs gave me no leeway so I simply had to endure their invasive leers.

I was relieved to be pushed into this new room for at least I was away form the prying eyes. The contents however filled my already pounding heart with dread because I knew that there would be nothing but misery for me in this place .

"Now, you little trollop, we're going to find out exactly what you were doing outside the camp the other night," said Banton threateningly.

"But I told you that I would talk," I stammered shocked at the possibility of more interrogation when I had already surrendered.

"You might tell me some things, but this device will ensure that you tell me everything," replied Banton unpleasantly.

With this she took me over to two metal poles that had various sinister looking gadgets attached to it. Electrical wires led away from the strange devices to sockets in the wall which seemed to explain the constant low hum in the room.

Once I was standing next to the contraption facing the chrome plated shaft Banton wasted no time in fastening me to it. She strapped my feet down slightly apart onto two levered pedals with the top of the shorter pole nestled between my thighs.

Banton began to turn a handle on the pole until the bulbous end was actually pressing against my vulva. When I realised what Banton was trying to do I started to panic but there was nothing I could do to foil her plans bound the way I was.

Halting only to pull my pussy lips apart to allow access to my vagina with her invading probe, she continued to turn the handle. And the more she turned it the higher the phallus went until it filled my sex completely.

Thankfully she eventually stopped when I was beginning to go up onto my toes to relieve the pressure inside me for it seemed as though I was being split in two. I pushed the levers on which I was standing back to the floor gingerly wondering all the while what other horrors she had in store for me.

Once she was satisfied with the impaling pole, Banton walked round to the other taller pole where she grasped two sinister looking crocodile clips with more wires trailing from them. As the intruding rod had made my nipples embarrassingly hard she had no trouble attaching the sharp toothed clamps to them.

The pain in my breasts was immediate and constant but this was not my only crisis for Banton threaded the wires over a pulley wheel at the top of the high pole. They were then fastened to a heavy metal weight that pulled the wires taut thus dragging my nipples painfully up into the air.

Mercifully the pointed weight dropped only a couple of inches to a metal ledge with even more wires running from it. This took some of the pressure from my nipples but I knew that there would be a catch to the temporary relief.

"At last we're ready," said Banton happily as she stood back to admire her handiwork.

"But there's no need to do anything else to me," I begged earnestly. "I will tell you everything you want to know, I promise."

"Yes, but let's be sure," smirked Banton. "Now you're not going to like this at all but at least it will help to ensure that you tell me the truth."

Banton proceeded to explain in loving detail what the machine was going to do to me once the electrical current was engaged.

"You see it's all to do with contacts," said Banton pointing to my feet and the large weight still resting on its ledge. "As long as you stand on your tiptoes and pull back with your breasts to keep this weight up, no contact is made."

I followed her finger nervously with my eyes, my mind racing with all the scary consequences of what she was saying.

"However, if you push down with your heels or let the weight drop then contact will be made and a powerful charge of electricity will pass through the clips and the large dildo inside you," said Banton gleefully. "It will be so painful that you will certainly not wish to get down off your toes again, unless that is you get too tired!"

"But please, Miss, I'll tell you the truth," I implored her. "Don't do this to me: I won't lie."

"Yes, my dear, I know you won't, but I also want to do this for my own pleasure," said Banton to my dismay. "And to stop your prattling I am going to gag you."

With that Banton produced a large red rubber ball with leather straps attached to it, which she proceeded to thrust into my mouth then fasten at the back of my neck. I was still able to make a lot of noise but cohesive words were completely beyond me.

"Now pull that weight up and get up on your dainty little toes because I am going to switch the current on now," ordered Banton as she walked over to the dreaded socket on the wall.

I struggled to comply as I stood on tiptoe and shifted my upper body back in order to pull the weight up from its bar. Once she saw that I was ready she flicked the switch that sent a hum of power flooding through the contraption which was going to torment me for God only knew how long.

"OK, you bitch, I'll come back in an hour or two to check that you're ready to tell me the truth," said Banton as she walked from the room. "And in the meantime keep on your toes or you'll soon know about it!"

A slam of the heavy door left me on my own with only a conveniently placed clock on the wall for me to look at. I arched my back as far as I could to keep the weight from making contact whilst trying to retain my balance perched on my toes.

I watched the seconds tick slowly by as the strain in my muscles began to tell with a gradual but inexorable build-up of pain. My calves and lower legs were already screaming their protests at my position but I dared not let myself drop down for fear of being fried by Banton's machine.

196

She had not put an exact time on her return but I already knew that I could not hold out for much longer especially with so little sleep the night before. Inevitably fatigue plus the increasing pain in my muscles led me to push my heels down slightly.

Instantly I was rewarded by a blast of electricity which slammed through my body causing me indescribable agony. My stomach felt like it had been kicked by a mule and I popped back up on my toes straight away but swung too far forward thus allowing the weight to make contact.

I yelled into my ball-gag as another bolt of power surged through every fibre of my being until I pulled the weight back up. This brought more anguish to my nipples because of the pressure on the clips but that was preferable to being shocked again.

I was in total misery, ready to admit to any crime that Banton cared to lay at my door but she did not come to hear my confession. I struggled on through the nightmare staring blindly at the clock trying to make time pass quicker to bring an end to my torment.

I lost count of the times that I slipped back on my heels or let the weight fail for the blasts of pain merged into a haze of misery. Tears streamed down my face but nobody came to ease my suffering so I laboured on alone. Eventually after what seemed like a life time of distress Banton came back grinning all over her malevolent face.

"I see that you have been having a lot of fun with my machine," she said walking up to me. "Now, when I take out your gag you will tell me the truth won't you or I will be forced to leave you like this for four hours next time."

Vigorously I nodded my head pleading dumbly with her to turn off the current .But she did not oblige for she wanted to question me whilst I was still exposed to the constant possibility of being shocked.

Shivering with fear I told Banton everything she wanted to know including all the other times that Bob had led us to investigate secret bases. I even told her of all my sexual encounters with Bob as well as all my other boyfriends each tit-bit of information interrupted by a jolt of electricity as I slipped from my precarious stance..

It was so humiliating but I wanted to be free of her dreadful machine so I let everything go even though I was incriminating my closest friends as well. Banton taped the whole conversation on a small tape recorder in her pocket until she was sure that she had drained me of absolutely everything.

Once she was satisfied she turned off the current whereupon I sank back onto the floor with my heels then let the weight drop once and for all. Silently she released me from her device of torture allowing me to fall to a sweating heap on the floor at her feet.

"Good girl, you have done well," said Banton bending down to stroke my matted hair. "Your story actually corroborates what your friends have already told Mires."

I shrank from her touch but she helped me to my feet explaining that I could now go with her to see them. Still handcuffed I followed her meekly, hoping all the while that she had not prepared more torture for me elsewhere in the labyrinth of endless corridors.

After a long walk Banton stopped at another grey door pausing only to open it for me before we both trooped in to see what fresh horrors had been created inside.

The first person we saw was Mires who turned to greet Banton with the news that the session was still going on as planned. She explained that something had to be done soon or the subjects would go mad with the frustration that was being created within them. As I looked past her I could see that the 'subjects' were my friends who were all bound cruelly to devices that were obviously responsible for their torment. Each one writhed in agony as whatever Mires was doing to them continued unabated.

All three were knelt tilting backwards with their backs to wooden boards which were about a yard square and resting a couple of feet off the floor on metal stands. My friends' arms were chained painfully over the tops of the boards whilst their legs had been folded then chained back under the boards.

They were completely naked apart from heavy leather hoods over their heads that were buckled tight behind them ensuring that they could neither see nor hear anything. Their thighs had been spread then bound to the wood with wide straps leaving them vulnerable to the other things that Mires had done to them.

I could see that Tia had a large black dildo stuffed up into her sex which was held in place with tight straps around her waist and between her swollen labia. Wires trailed from the visible end of the phallus as well as from crocodile clips firmly attached to the girl's trembling nipples.

I shivered as I remembered the experience I had just been through but I noticed that similar wires also led to the two boys' nipples. Between their splayed legs however were not dildos but glass tubes containing their rigid penises which seemed to pulsate before my very eyes. These were wired up like Tia's dildo then secured to their groins with similar leather straps.

The three friends had been muted with ball-gags as I had been but in addition they had electric wires attached to their temples with suckers. All the wires then led from the squirming prisoners to a bank of monitoring devices all topped with various screens feeding out an endless supply of information.

"They have told us everything that we need to know have

they?" asked Banton.

"Yes and it all seems to fit in with what cupcake there has told us," said Mires nodding at me.

"Well, I think it is time that she got to work again. This lot need some relief very quickly," said Banton.

"What do you mean?" I cried backing away from her.

"You see, my dear, we started torturing your friends whilst you were up on your toes," explained Banton. "And they sang like you did after we had put the juice through them for an hour or so."

"The juice?" I asked incredulously.

"Yes, they have had electrical currents passed constantly through their bodies via their nipples as well as the dildos that you can't see shoved up their asses," explained Banton.

"But why?" I asked thoroughly disturbed by the thought of anything pushed up inside my Bobby's rectum.

"The current stimulates the prisoners to the very point of orgasm then alerts us to the fact that they are about to come," continued Mires taking up the story. "Then the machine simply varies the current to deny them satisfaction."

"The same goes for the suction tubes on the boys' cocks," said Banton happily. They suck away until the lads are about to shoot their loads then they stop leaving them panting for more."

It was so brilliant that I simply stared at my poor friends as they suffered the endless torments of unrequited lust before me. No wonder they had revealed everything like I had in the vain hope of being allowed to experience their unreachable orgasms.

"But now that they've told us their secrets it's time for you to put them out of their misery," said Banton mischievously.

"What can I do?" I inquired naively.

"Oh, we know exactly what you can do," laughed Mires pointing to the heaving crotch of my boyfriend.

200

"No, you can't...not in front of you," I whimpered.

"Yes, we can," insisted Banton. "And if you don't you'll go back on your favourite electric device!"

Not wanting to go back into that particular room again I rushed up to where my boyfriend was bound and threw myself to my knees before him.

"Steady on, tiger," said Mires walking over to me. "We have to take the sucker tube off first then you can give him all you've got."

"And don't forget to swallow every bit of all that he has to give you," warned Banton.

Once Mires had removed the glass tube with its straps I got to work on the penis that I had lovingly sucked so many times in the past. It was so hard with the red blue veins almost at bursting point with the pressure from within.

I licked along the rampant shaft then took the bulbous end into my soft wet mouth with a contented sigh. Things were not so bad after all for this was what I loved to do for my Bobby if not exactly under these circumstances.

After a few brief sucks on his cock Bob went rigid then came in my mouth like a mini pressure hose. The torrent of warm sticky semen flowed down my throat like a waterfall whilst he moaned into his gag with delight above me.

Once I had swallowed every drop of his precious fluid I turned to face my captors who were both laughing at me. I did not care because I had brought some satisfaction to my beloved Bobby who was now free of the never ending torment he had suffered before.

"Well done, you little whore," said Banton. "I can see you're no beginner."

"No and imagine how the other two feel, still writhing in torment beside your boyfriend," said Mires. "Don't they deserve the same treatment?"

"But, I couldn't..."

"That's what you said last time and the punishment is still the same if you don't chew that bitch out and suck his cock as well," snarled Banton. "So get on with it, now!"

The thought of licking Tia's pussy revolted me initially, especially with this sadistic audience. But I had serviced my new mistresses' sexes without too much difficulty plus I liked Tia very much and she was in desperate need of some satisfaction.

I had no choice in the matter so I steeled myself for the task ahead whilst I shuffled over between Tia's twitching legs. Mires did not bother to remove Tia's dildo So I simply leant forward so that I could part Tia's trembling labia then find her swollen clitoris. I lapped at the hardened flesh with quick expert strokes until Tia also came flooding my salt filled mouth with her delicious juices which trickled down the sides of the dildo embedded deep within her.

As she screamed with sheer relief overhead I decided to induce yet another orgasm for her in the wake of the first one. I bit down roughly on her clit thus sending her off into a series of uncontrollable convulsions as multiple orgasms rocked her entire frame.

"Oh, very generous, you tart," said Banton realising what I had done. "I am sure she'll be grateful to you when she eventually calms down."

"Now for Richie," laughed Mires pointing at his straining member in its glass prison.

"But..."

"Don't even think about it," said Banton. "Just get on with it!"

As Mires removed Richie's tube I moved over between his legs which constantly thrust his pelvis forward in the hopeless search for an orgasm. His cock was not as big as Bobby's but it had grown as big as it possibly could under the relentless influence of the glass tube.

I stuck out my tongue tentatively but knowing that Bob was unable to see me I soon became bolder. I was fascinated to discover what Richie tasted like so I caressed his rod with my tongue with long lavish strokes.

Richie reacted with groans of delight as he realised that he might have the chance to come at last. He pushed himself forward in an effort to shove his penis into my mouth so I decided to oblige by parting my lips to let him in.

The distinctive flavour of Richie's pre-ejaculate filled my mouth as I began to suck on his trembling cock. If anything I felt he was even saltier than Bobby which was confirmed when he exploded in my mouth almost causing me to choke.

I gulped down his semen as quickly as I could to give me a chance to breathe but I also made sure that I lapped up every drop even when I pulled my head back. Dutifully I cleaned his cock thoroughly before struggling back to my feet.

"Excellent, you put on a great show," cried Mires clapping her hands at my efforts. "Look at the three of them - all relaxed now that you have saved them from their own frustration."

"That's right Mires, now take their masks off and show them who was responsible," ordered Banton with a nasty look in my direction.

Mires removed the hoods from my friends who each looked at me in turn with looks of total surprise. Even when they were free of their ball-gags none of them could speak until Bob finally pulled himself together.

"How could you Sandy, in front of these people?" he asked, astonished to find that I had been their saviour.

"I had no choice, Bobby," I whimpered as he glowered at me.

"And the others?" he continued quietly.

I could do nothing but nod my head in shame especially as he looked away in disgust at this latest twist to our misfortune.

"Yes, you little slut, you did the job so well that you should do this for a living," said Banton bitchily. "You could make a fortune on your knees or on your back come to think of it."

"You made me do it," I yelled, guilty at what I had done. "It was either that or the damn electric pole and I couldn't stand that again."

"I know, my dear," smirked Baton. "Life's a bitch and so am I but you're the ones in chains and I'm the one with the power to let you go."

"You mean we can go now?" I said doubtfully.

"Yes, you can thanks to the information you all gave us as well as what you did for these ungrateful sods, "said Mires as she began to release the others from their bonds.

"You will be flown back to the airfield you left two days ago and then we don't want to hear any more from you," continued Banton. "If you come back or mention your adventure to anyone we will know and we will come after you."

"And what will you do to us then?" demanded Bob with a trace of defiance still in his voice.

"Well you saw that little CIA girl," said Banton threateningly. "She came back again after we released her - now she will never leave. She will serve our top brass on her knees for the rest of her days."

"But you can't..." spluttered Bob.

"Oh but I can and will," insisted Banton. "Get out of my sight and don't let me catch you again or I'll make the things you have endured so far seem like a walk in the park!"

With that Banton opened a cupboard where our tattered clothes had been stored then left Mires to unchain us so that we could get dressed. We quickly pulled on what was left of our jump suits on then followed Mires out of the underground bunker that had been our home for the last couple of days.

Outside we were surprised to find that is was the middle of the night but we were given no time to look around. We were herded into a Blackhawk helicopter which whisked us away back over the Nevada border to the tiny airstrip we had taken off from less than fifty hours before.

Once there we were unceremoniously dumped from the helicopter which then headed back the way we had come.

"Well, that's that ." I sighed as we watched the helicopter depart.

"Oh, I don't know," said Bob. "Don't you want to find out more?"

"But what about the things Banton did to us?" I demanded. "She'll do it again you know and next time it'll be much worse!"

"Well, there's only one way to find out..."

And now for the opening of next months title "TOMB OF PAIN" by Arabella Lancaster-Symes

Chapter One

Lady Susan Quinn moved regally through the enormous, luxuriously appointed room, nodding to acquaintances, pausing to speak and to share a joke with this person or that.

The party was going quite well, and she was sure donations for the new Opera House would be generous from those in attendance. It would be quite a coup over that wretched cow Nellie Parkinson at their next.

She froze, the blood slowly draining from her face as she caught sight of the two women standing together in the lee of a marble column. Erika Wolf looked striking in a tall, black, mannish suit, her short, dark hair barely brushing the collar. And beside her, their heads almost indecently close as they whispered, was Susan's daughter Hannah.

Hannah was eighteen, a striking young woman with calm, intelligent, self-assured blue eyes. Her golden hair was parted at the centre of her forehead, framing her delicately boned face perfectly and falling to either side like purest spun silk to dangle just across the shoulders of her forest green dress.

Half the women in the room had paid fortunes to achieve the particular perfection of colour in Hannah's hair, and the rest had gone to plastic surgeons to achieve the beauty of her small, graceful nose, her full, sensuous lips, or that impossibly perfect, barely perceptible cleft in her chin. None of them had succeeded with what nature had done so casually with Hannah though.

Looking at Hannah never failed to fill Susan with pride - until now. Now she stood rigidly as the guests moved around her, staring at her daughter with Erika Wolf. She watched the tall, German woman's finger slide slowly along the nape of Hannah's neck, then ease down her chest between the swellings of her high, firm breasts.

Hannah blushed slightly, and then she and Erika laughed.

And the room dissolved around her as Susan recalled her last meeting with Erika, two years earlier. She had just divorced her husband. An attractive woman, Susan was blonde, like her daughter, and in the latter part of her thirties still slim-hipped. Her small breasts were still firm and well-shaped and she was reasonably content with the way she looked. She had been sexually repressed during her marriage, and had thought to engage in a little daring exploration.

But Erika Wolf was not one to experiment with. You did not dabble with Erika Wolf. For she took you by the scruff of the neck and yanked you in all the way.

Her first night had been spent trying to hold back screams of pleasure as Erika had shown her something her husband never had, an expertise at cunnilingus which had left her writhing and straining and convulsing on the bed to the point of dazed stupefaction.

It had seemed too natural, and, of course, wickedly daring, to let Erika tie her wrists and ankles to the corner posts. It would keep her in place and stop her shaking around. And so it had. But the binding had done something more, something to her mind. It had freed her of the need to act, to participate, to even think about what was happening. It had opened up her submissive side, the side which wanted, yearned to submit to another, stronger personality.

Erika had drawn her into her web quickly, first with spankings and small, almost playful slaps, then light switchings, strappings, the cane...

It was in Erika's townhouse that she had come to the end of her experimentation. She had fallen well under Erika's spell by then.

Her head had been fitted with a heavy leather hood which covered her entirely save for two small eye holes and another over her mouth. A ball gag was stuffed deep into her mouth, the strap going around her head and fastening behind her. A thick collar covered her slender neck, and dangling from its rear were two strong straps. Susan's wrists had been forced painfully high up behind her back and locked into those straps, and, wearing nothing else save a pair of stiletto heels, she had been led into a room which contained several of her more notable acquaintances.

Shocked, horrified, she had tried to draw back, but could not. She had seen the arousal in their eyes, and felt shame and panic flooding her even as she realized they did not know who she was.

Lyndon Saunders, her husband's business partner, Lord Peter Bailey, husband of Veronica Bailey, one of her best friends, and Liam Walker, a man she literally despised for his foul mouth and arrogant nouveau riche behaviour stood and looked at her and licked their lips with the anticipation of pleasure.

And she could not move for fear of somehow giving away her identity. Erika led her forward, holding a narrow chain leash which separated at its end to clip tightly onto both of Susan's aching, throbbing nipples.

"What do you think of my little pet, gentlemen?" Erika said in a throaty purr.

"Lovely little piece of it," Walker said, his coarse voice hungry.

Bailey reached over and slid his hand up to cover one of her breasts, then squeezed cruelly. She groaned in pain as his fingers worked into the sensitive flesh.

"Come, dog," Erika said, yanking on the leash.

Her nipples burned and Susan threw herself after the woman, whimpering as she was led against a low chair and forced to bend far over and spread her legs. The knowledge of how lewdly she was displayed before the three men shamed her to the core, and she only prayed Erika did nothing to reveal her identity.

Fingers slid along her soft, perfectly shaved slit, then a buzzing filled the air. She whimpered a denial but could do nothing as Erika ran the tip of the vibrator up and down her pussy.

She had never felt a vibrator before Erika had introduced them to her, and she had fallen well and truly in love with them. Now as it ground over her clitoris, she felt the heat of sexual arousal seeping through her lower body, and moaned in shame.

Then the penetration. It was a large vibrator, and Erika was not gentle. She thrust it into Susan's aching pussy, forcing aside the soft flesh to all but bury it within her quivering cavity.

And then she had strapped her, strapped her powerfully, until she was sobbing and crying into the gag.

And yet, despite the pain, and humiliation, or possibly with their aid, a small and frightened part of her

210

thought, her arousal only deepened, and her pussy squeezed down hungrily on the vibrator within it as the strap turned her backside a glowing red.

Erika pulled her upright so quickly she was dizzy, then pushed her to her knees before the three men. All of them were nude now, and Susan blanched at their full erections. She felt Erika undo the strap of her gag, and knew panic again as she pried the ball from her lips.

They can't know me! They can't! I'll be destroyed!

Yet there was no sign of recognition in their eyes as Erika pulled her up off her heels and Walker reached down to grasp her head and feed her his cock.

Her mouth opened reluctantly, but, she realized with shock, some degree of hunger, as well. Her lower belly thrummed with lewd excitement as she fed on his hot, fat prick. She began to suck as Erika had taught her, for this was not the first man the German woman had given her to.

"Ahh, yes," he groaned, holding her head between his strong hands. "Suck me, you filthy little slut!"

Fear made her shudder again, yet a secret delight set her thighs closing to squeeze together excitedly. They didn't know who she was! They had no idea!

Her lips bobbed up and down on his thick cock as he looked down at her, then he began to thrust into her, using her as a masturbatory tool, forcing his cock into her throat as Erika had previously done with strap-on dildos.

He used her throat then, thrusting deep, burying every inch of his lance within her as he jerked her face back and forth against his groin. He gasped and came, pouring his semen down her throat and softening almost instantly.

211

It was Bailey's turn, and he drew over a heavy chair to sit comfortably, beckoning her forward. She leaned in between his legs and took him into her mouth, bending at the waist. And cried out weakly as Erika began caning her bottom.

The pain was terrible, but the pleasure even more so, and her buttocks began to roll in helpless, wanton heat as her lips bobbed up and down on Bailey's cock. Her entire bottom was on fire now, a deep, scorching conflagration which seemed to absorb the pain of every new blow and defuse it. Then that heat seeped into her belly and joined with the wondrous heat there, and she knew she was near to losing herself.

"Take her!"

She heard the words through a haze, her lips sucking hungrily on Bailey's cock. She hardly noticed Saunders move behind her, nor felt his touch at first. Then as his stiff erection slipped along her thigh she realized he was about to mount her and a fresh flood of liquid heat oozed down around the vibrator.

It was only when he began to work his staff into her rectum that she recognized his intent, and momentarily struggled to break free.

They held her easily, and her will dissolved. Yet another "disgusting" activity she had refused to partake in was about to occur, and she no longer had the will to resist.

Saunders drove himself into her hard and deep, and she shuddered with the pain inside her. But another part of her gloried in her own degradation, in yet another reduction of her proud self to the status of cheap, sluttish tart.

His hands squeezed and kneaded her breasts crudely, tugging on the leash to yank the clips against her nipples. She whimpered and moaned around Bailey's cock, but continued to work her lips up and down as Saunders slowly filled her backside with his long, thick erection.

He sodomized her. What a crude, disgusting word for a crude, disgusting act, she thought dazedly. Her insides ached as his big cock pumped back and forth, and yet - the revulsion she felt turned and twisted into that same terrible delight at her own humiliation and degradation.

And so Lady Susan Quinn, famous for her regal bearing, her sharp wits, her pride and steady, unflappable nature, sucked frenziedly on Bailey's cock as Saunders raped her anus with savage gusto. And then she dissolved into the maelstrom of a wonderful and terrible climax.

Her body sizzled from head to toe, and her insides squirmed and twisted. Her mind soared to unbearable heights as the pleasure clawed at her and tore her sense of self to shreds. Nothing mattered but this pleasure. Nothing! She felt now the attraction of addiction, knew how those dirty people in the city could scuttle along alleys, caring for nothing but feeding their addiction.

For this was her addiction, and nothing on Earth mattered to her compared to the elation and ecstasy she felt while gripped within its embrace.

When it was over and they had emptied their seed into her trembling, shaking body, they dragged her to a post and beat her again, and again, then made her masturbate with two gigantic dildos while they watched. She crawled before them, the two dildos painfully straining her anus and pussy, licking at their feet like an animal.

A part of her was frightened. She was losing all con-

213

trol of herself. But at that moment she really had no care but to satisfy the terrible lust within her.

Susan shook herself free of the memory with a tremendous effort of will. That had been the last time she had given in to the lust. She had refused to meet with Erika again, had refused to partake in anything with the woman. She had returned to her prim, proper upbringing.

Every time she met one of those three men again - and she had done so many times, she had felt a deep sense of shame, but also a sense of emptiness.

And there was Erika Wolf. With her sweet Hannah.

Her stomach twisted to see the woman's fingers on her daughter's soft, ivory skin. Hannah's head turned away briefly, and Susan saw the calculating look in Erika's eyes as they examined the shapely young blonde girl's body.

An image came into Susan's head unbidden, of Hannah nude and bound at Erika's feet, being given to men, used, and degraded.

She moved forward, throwing the image off, striding angrily across the room, ignoring voices calling out to her until she stood before the two.

Hannah looked up in surprise, smiling.

"Mother, this is..."

"I know who this is, Hannah. Go into the salon and see how Jeffrey is doing."

Hannah blinked and turned to look at Erika.

"Now," Susan snapped.

Hannah glared at the unaccustomed command in her mother's voice. She was not a girl who took to being ordered about. Still, she was not a girl to make a scene without reason either. She would inform her mother of her displeasure later. She turned and left, and Susan turned to Erika.

"How have you been, Susie?" Erika asked.

Susan flinched. "My name is Susan. I don't believe you were on the invitation list for this event, Erika."

"Lord Saunders invited me. You remember he and I are acquainted."

Susan felt her face heating.

"I suggest you leave."

"Why? I'm not doing any harm. I was merely chatting with that delicious looking young girl you sent away. I had no idea she was your daughter."

She sipped delicately from the crystal goblet in her hand.

"Delightful girl, quite intelligent and beautiful."

"You stay away from Hannah!" Susan hissed.

Erika gave her a disappointed look. "Now, Susie, I never did anything to you that you didn't want done. You wanted to throw off your prudish past and experiment and so you did. Perhaps little Hannah wants the same."

"I told you... if you go near her I'll..."

"You'll what?" Erika demanded in a low, smug voice. "You'll crawl before me and beg for forgiveness? You'll tell everyone what an evil slut I am for giving you more orgasms in a day than you had in your entire previous life?"

Erika eased forward and Susan took an unwilling step back.

"No, my dear. Don't even try to threaten me. If I want your pretty little daughter I shall have her. I'll teach her

215

how to pleasure a woman, then give her to every man I can find."

Susan's face burned with fury, but she dared not speak. Those around them were already looking curious, and she had far more to lose than Erika.

"When I make her sing for me, darling, I'll tape it and send you the song in the post. She has a sweet contralto voice. I'm sure it will soar when I have her spread-eagled on a bed and writhing in pleasure.

"Just like her mother's did."

Chapter Two

Jessica blinked her eyes to see the sun rising outside her window, and gasped as she jerked her head up. It was well past five, and she was not close to finished the special assignment Ms. Wolf had given her! She tried to draw her scattered wits together and throw off the haze of sexual need which had followed her into waking. She reached to her breasts, squeezing lightly through her dress, then lowered one hand between her legs, rubbing herself there as she felt her arousal quickening.

Sleep had come over her swiftly, and with it a fantasy, just as unbidden, a fantasy involving Ms. Wolf, her Archaeology teacher. Why she was continuing to have these sexual fantasies involving Wolf was beyond her. Jessica, at nineteen, had never seriously considered the idea of sex with another woman. In fact, coming from a Catholic school, and bound up in her studies, she rarely considered sex at all.

But the woman was so utterly sensuous, so powerful and strong, both physically and intellectually. She had impressed Jessica the moment she'd seen her, and the fantasies had started shortly thereafter, fantasies she had found deeply disturbing, at first, but was helpless to prevent.

How did women have sex, anyway? Her mind provided strange scenes of writhing flesh, of mouths on breasts and hands on rounded buttocks. Sick! Yet helplessly arousing!

What would a woman like Wolf be like in bed? Would she be cold and formal? Surely not! Perhaps that perfect dignity with which she always seemed to surround herself would give way in the arms of her lover and she would become soft and passionate.

Jessie blinked her eyes in the sudden glare as the sun rose over the trees, her left hand fumbling at the buttons down the front of her dress and her right tugging up her hem to slide beneath.

She slumped back somewhat, breathing more heavily, her left hand dipping into the cup of her bra to fondle her hot, sparkling nipple while her right eased down the front of her panties and stroked along the narrow gulley between her pubic lips.

She groaned aloud, chest rising and falling faster now as her fingers moved rapidly over her clitoris. Her head came back farther and farther, her legs spreading wide. Her index finger sought the small, tight entrance to her body, then wriggled up inside as her thumb stroked with growing desperation against the swollen little button above.

She closed her eyes against the light, seeing Ms. Wolf, imagining it was her hands upon her body, her fingers setting the fires roaring inside her. Eyes closed, her lips

217

formed into kisses and she thought, for a brief moment, she could feel Ms. Wolf's own lips upon them.

Then her body jerked sharply, head going back much further as she arched her back. Her buttocks ground into the hard chair beneath as the climax came over her and swept her mind into a torrent of unrestrained pleasure.

She groaned and went limp, panting for breath, eyes slowly blinking open as her hands relaxed beneath her dress. She spent a few minutes recovering her composure, then straightened herself and set about finishing the essay in a manner which would impress Ms. Wolf.

She felt a little faint when she finally stood up, and far from confident she had what Wolf would consider an appropriate summation. Time was gone, however, for any alterations. Wolf had only grudgingly permitted her this attempt to make up for a poor exam grade, and it must be handed in early, before Wolf's first class.

She gazed down at her dress, then chewed unknowingly on her lip once more. This would certainly not do. It was, according to her clock, quarter to seven. However, she had set it forward a good quarter hour two months before to prevent herself being late for classes. So she had the time to clean up a bit.

She reached behind her and quickly unfastened her dress. It was a simple garment, for, when away from her parents, she was not much given to fripperies. She stripped it off and stepped out of it, moving quickly to her wardrobe.

She took down her green dress, for it set off her soft, wavy chestnut hair so nicely, and slipped into it. She decided it was too formal. She removed it and drew on a white one, pretty, and somewhat short (for her), and quickly buttoned it up before turning to the mirror.

"Damn," she said deliberately.

She removed the elastic which had bound her shoulder length hair back in a loose tail and brushed at it furiously, working at the bangs to get just the right look, brushing it out so it tumbled glossily over her shoulders.

Finally, glancing at the clock, she sighed and grabbed her papers. Ms. Wolf was a fanatic about punctuality, and she couldn't risk being a single minute late.

She cut across the south common, and in her haste failed to notice the hose snaking its way along the grass to the sprinkler sweeping water back and forth. Her ankle caught on the hose at the top of a low hillock and she went flying forward, the report spilling from her hands. She wound up on her stomach in the wet grass and dirt, her skirt up around her waist. She lay stunned a moment, water raining down on her, then scrambled to her knees with a cry of dismay, shoving her skirt back down. She stared around wildly, then snatched at the nearest paper, already somewhat damp. She twisted and snatched at another, then crawled to a third, hurriedly lifting them and holding them protectively beneath her chest as the water continued to patter down onto her back and head.

With the last of them in hand she scrambled out of range of the sprinkler, and stood still, panting for breath and staring down at the wet papers, the ink already running in numerous places. Water was trickling down her cheeks as well, and in a moment, she knew, her tears would join it.

There was no time to return and change, not without further provoking Ms. Wolf by being late. She hurried on, hoping her explanation would do, and the woman would be a little sympathetic to her bedraggled appearance.

The building which housed the comfortable flats provided to unmarried professors who chose to stay on campus was only a few hundred feet along, and she was soon tugging the heavy door aside and trotting up the stairs.

She was breathless as she reached the door to Ms. Wolf's apartment but she was on time - she thought, though she had cut it quite close despite her best intentions.

There was no answer to her knock, and, chewing lightly on her lip, she knocked again, louder. She was about to knock for a third time when Ms. Wolf opened the door.

"McMann," she said, her voice cold.

Jessie was caught by her own surprise at sight of the woman. She wore a long robe, and her heart beat faster at the thought of what lay beneath.

"Ms. Wolf," Jessie whispered, clutching the papers to her chest.

"What time did I set for the delivery of your report?" she demanded, ignoring the water dripping from her hair.

Jessie blinked in surprise. "Seven, Miss."

"Seven. Not quarter past seven."

"But... but I'm quite certain I'm on time!" Jessie exclaimed desperately.

"You're quite certainly wrong then," the woman said with a scowl.

"But I..."

Then she remembered how Anne Baxter had been toying with the clock the other day, and her heart sank as she realized the girl might well have reset it to its proper time, all unknowing why it was fast. She hurriedly attempted to explain, but Wolf appeared less than impressed.

"If you can't manage punctuality here in the school, McMann, how do you intend to do so in a future career?"

"Please, Ms. Wolf I - "

"Pleas are for beggars and children. Which are you?"

"Ms. Wolf - "

"What have you done to yourself?" Wolf looked at her dirty dress in disgust and Jessie felt on the verge of tears.

"Oh, never mind. Get inside, girl," she said crossly.

Jessie bit her lip and stepped inside, her eyes quickly darting around, thrilled, despite the situation, at being in Ms. Wolf's very own rooms.

There was a comfortable looking sofa facing a small fireplace, and lovely curtains over the window. She wondered if Ms. Wolf had made them herself, for they did not look store bought. To one side was a narrow table of some dark, polished wood, with a sculpture of some sort atop it. Past the living room was an open door she thought must surely lead into the bedroom, and her heart beat quicker at the sight.

"How, McMann, do you expect to make your way about the world if you cannot get across the campus?"

Jessie tried to explain about the clock, and the sprinkler, her words tumbling over themselves before Wolf silenced her with two fingers against her lips.

"I don't want to hear it. You're babbling like a child, McMann."

She gazed at Jessie for a long moment without speaking.

To be continued..........

The cover photograph for this book and many others are
available as limited edition prints.
Write to:-

Viewfinders Photography
PO Box 200,
Reepham
Norfolk
NR10 4SY

for details, or see,

www.viewfinders.org.uk

All titles are available as electronic downloads at:

http://www.electronicbookshops.com

e-mail submissions to:
Editor@electronicbookshops.com

STILETTO TITLES

1-897809-99-9   Maria's Fulfillment *Jay Merson*
1-897809-98-0   The Rich Bitch *Becky Ball*
1-897809-97-2   Slaves of the Sisterhood *Anna Grant*
1-897809-96-4   Stocks and Bonds *John Angus*
1-897809-94-8   Mistress Blackheart *Francine Whittaker*
1-897809-93-X   Military Discipline *Anna Grant*

Due for release March 20th 2001
1-897809-92-1   Tomb of Pain *Arabella Lancaster-Symes*

Due for release April 20th 2001
1-897809-91-3   Slave Training Academy *Paul James*

Due for release May 20th 2001
1-897809-90-5   Submission to Desire *A. Lancaster-Symes*

Due for release June 20th 2001
1-897809-89-1   The Governess *Serena Di Frisco*

Due for release July 20th 2001
1-897809-88-3   Stern Manor *Denise la Criox*

Due for release August 20th 2001
1-897809-87-5   Six of the Best (Anthology) *Various*